A GUARD DOG NAMED HONEY

A GUARD DOG NAMED HONEY

Denise Gosliner Orenstein

SCHOLASTIC PRESS / NEW YORK

Library of Congress Cataloging-in-Publication Data

Names: Orenstein, Denise Gosliner, 1950– author.
Title: A guard dog named Honey / Denise Orenstein.
Description: First edition. | New York: Scholastic Press, 2020. | Audience: Ages 8–12 | Summary:
When her older brother is arrested on her eleventh birthday, Bean Wright is devastated, and determined
to raise the bail money that their mother does not have; the most promising scheme she comes up with is
getting a young girl named Phoebe, one of the summer residents, to sell her valuable Mastiff guard dog,
Honey—but the scheme takes a dark turn when the buyer turns out to want Honey for dog fighting.
Identifiers: LCCN 2019025353 (print) | LCCN 2019025354 (ebook) |
ISBN 9781338348460 (hardcover) | ISBN 9781338348507 (ebook other)
Subjects: LCSH: Mastiff—Juvenile fiction. | Dogfighting—Juvenile fiction. | Brothers and sisters—
Juvenile fiction. | Mothers and daughters—Juvenile fiction. | Single-parent families—Juvenile fiction. |
Friendship—Juvenile fiction. | CYAC: Mastiff—Fiction. | Dogs—Fiction. | Brothers and sisters—
Fiction. | Mothers and daughters—Fiction. | Single-parent families—Fiction. | Friendship—Fiction.
Classification: LCC PZ7.O6314 Gu 2020 (print) | LCC PZ7.O6314 (ebook) |
DDC 813.54 [Fic]—dc23
LC record available at https://lccn.loc.gov/2019025353
LC ebook record available at https://lccn.loc.gov/2019025354

10 9 8 7 6 5 4 3 2 1   20 21 22 23 24

Printed in the U.S.A.   23

First edition, March 2020

Book design by Yaffa Jaskoll

For Mimi Trotta, beloved friend

Until one has loved an animal, a part of
one's soul remains unawakened.

—Anatole France

PART ONE

DOWN UNDER

CHAPTER ONE

My brother was arrested on my eleventh birthday.

Sheriff Ernestine Cobbs showed up at our door, just as we were sitting down to cut into my tutti-frutti three-layer cake, the kind my mother made me every year. She always hid gummy bears in each layer, and back when we were little kids, Willis and I fought over the biggest slice.

Now Willis is grown, almost seventeen. He's tall and skinny—"Just real fit, not skinny, sis," he'd insist whenever I teased him about his bony frame. My brother is straight-up handsome, unlike the friends who slouched alongside him, their faces dotted with gross pimples, their eyes half-closed, thin mouths clamped into sneers. Willis stood above the rest, his shoulders squared, head held high, his tanned face smooth as the lagoon water down the road from our house, and his eyes that same bluish-green lagoon color too. He was usually smiling or laughing, but not in a wannabe way. Willis wore his face like someone who knew what was up and was happy about it.

So when Sheriff Cobbs knocked and the three of us noticed her broad hat and small frame through the battered screen door, I saw Willis's eyes narrow. My brother stood up quickly. His fork clattered to the floor.

"Ernestine, please," my mother said slowly. "Now's not the time. It's Bean's birthday."

Three green cans of Mountain Dew trembled on the kitchen counter. The pile of dirty dishes in the sink shifted. A rubber band in my mother's hand snapped.

The vinegar scent of sweat filled the air.

I don't remember how long it took for the sheriff to clip Willis's wrists into handcuffs or if anyone said anything more. The afternoon slowly turned a weepy green, right inside my birthday kitchen, a yellowish, pukish green just like the rain clouds outside.

I might have gotten kinda dizzy then, kinda wobbly on my feet as the sheriff led Willis slowly out the door. Reaching for the back of a kitchen chair to steady myself, I stumbled, then sat down quickly. My mother looked at me blankly, then poured a glass of water from the sink into an old jelly jar.

"Doing okay, Bean? You don't look so great."

"Feels like the room's moving all around," I whispered. "Feels like I'm getting sick."

"Coming down with something? Maybe a cold?"

I shook my head, which didn't help matters one bit. My mother seemed so cool and collected, as if Willis's arrest had never happened. Of course I wasn't feeling okay and it wasn't because of a stupid cold. "Kind of like everything's spinning."

"Feeling dizzy?"

I nodded. The room heaved and then dipped like a boat.

"Vertigo," my mother said softly, handing me the water.

"You look pale as all get out. I used to get it myself from time to time after your father left."

"What's vertigo?" My voice sounded hollow, as if coming from a deep tunnel, from far away.

"It means losing your balance," my mother said. "It's the sense that your world has turned upside down. Like everything around you is moving and just won't stop. Put your head down for a second, Bean, and drink up. That should do the trick."

So I laid my head down on the square oak table in front of me and closed my eyes. Our house was so small that the living room and kitchen were really just one room, and we used the old table for most everything—eating, cooking, folding clothes, studying, painting projects, and more. The scratched-up wood surface felt rough against my cheek, so I sat up slowly again, then drank the cold water in two large gulps. Blurry plywood walls and squat windows came back into focus, and the floor steadied. But when I turned to tell my mother that I felt better, I saw that she was washing dishes left from break-fast, the rush of water from the faucet so loud that I knew she wouldn't be able to hear me.

CHAPTER TWO

I live on Rock Haven Island in Massachusetts, a place known for pretty beaches and as a fancy summer vacation spot. Most think Rock Haven is just for the rich and famous, for their giant gray-shingled houses with winding, endless porches. Come Memorial Day, these folks begin jamming our ferries or flying right on island in private planes. Sometimes there's even a yacht or two docked in Rock Haven's main harbor. Once, I saw one with a French flag at its mast. But most who visit Rock Haven for a vacation never even know where the real islanders live. And it's not in those mansions perched at the ocean's edge, I can tell you that.

Real islanders, not the wealthy and not the wash ashores, have called Rock Haven home for years and years. Fishermen, construction workers, teachers, shopkeepers, nurses, police officers, and regular folks like that. We have what Willis calls a cool hodgepodge population: African Americans, Wampanoag Native Americans, Portuguese, Jamaicans, Brazilians, Whites, and more have long histories on island, making it a pretty interesting place. Last spring, the town council voted us a sanctuary community, meaning anyone in need, anyone from anywhere, could come live here at any time. No questions asked.

And us islanders stick it out together, no matter what—during the winters, no matter how cold the winds and no matter how deep the snow. We don't pack our bags and leave just as the weather is getting rough. Rock Haven is our home in every single season, whatever comes our way.

Unless they're like my father. He used to head to what we called America whenever he got a chance. (Of course, we all knew that Rock Haven is a part of the United States of America, but most of us felt so different, so far away from the mainland cities and towns, that it seemed more like we were living in an entirely separate country, or our own separate continent.)

"There's more work off island," my mother always told me. "Your father's just trying to help support all of us."

Funny, it seemed that my father slowly faded from our lives until one day, about a year ago, he decided to not ever come back to Rock Haven or to us. Maybe he found another family somewhere in America, another daughter and son. Maybe he just got sick of island life and sick of us too. My mother told Willis and me that our father couldn't hack living in such a remote place. "It's real hard to make a decent living here," she said, avoiding our eyes. "We'll be fine. Just wait and see. He'll still send us money, whenever he finds good work."

That's when my hives first started. Round red spots that itched like crazy and came and went with no warning. But I didn't tell anyone about them except for my brother. I didn't want anyone else to know.

Willis promised me that the hives were only temporary and

that they'd disappear once I got older and learned how to deal. I didn't exactly know what that meant but was glad that I wouldn't be covered with the itchy things forever.

And what I also didn't understand was this: What did my mother mean about "a decent living"? And how the heck can a family live "decently" when the father's gone? But I guess we did. We managed kinda okay, my mother, Willis, and I.

At least I thought we did.

Our little house was crammed in along with a bunch of others on the lagoon side of the island. Low slung, paint worn off, one-story frame houses battered with age and bad weather. On narrow streets without sidewalks, clumps of beach grass growing out of the concrete, old cars and trailers hunched together on sandy slivers of lawn. Peeling skiffs and rowboats, their wooden frames shaped like crooked smiles; rusted pails; car wheels; tin cans; and sometimes an old doll, painted face worn off. Stones, pebbles, oily fish skeletons, and fading seashells.

But where others might see old junk, Willis and I noticed bits of colors in all those worn and broken things, and where others might see sad and ugly, my brother taught me to make out the bright, speckled shape of our island home. The sparkle of mica in rocks and the jade green of crushed shell rot. My brother would point out all this to me so that I'd always see the best in everything. But after he was arrested that became pretty hard.

My mother has worked at the Rock Haven Stop & Shop

supermarket for over fifteen years, long before I was even born. She could usually be found at the first-aisle cash register in her stiff dark-green uniform, wearing her name tag with NELL WRIGHT printed in black letters, chatting it up with anyone who came her way. She'd always be right there during those crazy-busy times in the summer, when she "hardly has a minute to breathe," and also in the slow times during the winter when I've seen her huddled out front in the cold with Sally Owens and Jake Cobbs (the sheriff's husband), drinking coffee out of paper cups and shooting the breeze. Sometimes she'd see me and yell, "Get yourself home right now, Bean Wright! It's getting late and you should be doing your homework with your brother."

Fat chance. Willis and I never did our homework until the last minute, long after my mother got home. We'd sit together at the old oak table and watch her warm up an extra bowl of ramen noodle soup or make us grilled cheese sandwiches for a late-evening snack. Then Willis would pull out his thick books from his backpack and quiet would fall.

This was my favorite time of day, when I got to sit right next to my brother, neither of us saying much of anything but still together. The sound of Willis's pencil scratching away on lined paper and the sight of his large, knobby hands clutching a book were comforting to me, and it was the only time I got my brother all to myself, without his girlfriends or tagalongs. But I really didn't care for books, although I was pretty good at math. Somehow anything with numbers made sense to me.

"Wake up and smell the coffee, little dudette," my brother would say to me when my eyes would start to close those long evenings. "Can't go to sleep until all your homework is done." And so I'd try to stay awake and finish every assignment, read every handout, and answer every question on every take-home test. I never wanted to disappoint Willis.

The night of my eleventh birthday, the winds started up right after Sheriff Cobb took Willis in handcuffs to jail. Then came the hard rain, the horizontal kind. My mother and I stood by the window, where we watched the sky widen, spreading its bruised chest.

"Some birthday," my mother said, her hand on my back.

I nodded.

"Try not to worry too much, Bean. You know that this has been coming for a long time. Almost a relief. At least I'll know where he is nights." Then my mother turned to the old table, still set for my birthday, the cake tilted to one side where Willis had stuck in a finger on the hunt for gummy bears. She glanced back at me with a weak smile. "I'll go down to the jail first thing in the morning and see if I can rustle up the money for bail, but let's not count on it."

My mother looked old then; her whole face drooped as if it didn't have any bones to hang itself on. Her hazel eyes sunk, her mouth sagged at the corners, and her complexion turned ash. But it was only for a minute. Soon, she looked like my mother again. She combed her straight salt-and-pepper hair with her fingers, then gathered it into the rubber band that she always wore on her wrist. Her hands shook.

I started to walk away toward my bedroom, but when she called me, I turned back. My mother was pretty tall, almost as tall as Willis, and she had the same broad shoulders and wiry frame. She was wearing a pair of blue jeans rolled up at the ankles and her favorite black-and-green flannel shirt, the wrist cuffs soggy with dishwater. Neither of us moved for a minute.

"It will be okay, Bean," she finally whispered into the air, then repeated to herself in a louder voice, "It will be okay if I can get the bail cash."

I wasn't exactly sure what bail was, but I did know that "rustling up" cash wasn't going to be easy. There was barely extra money for everyday things.

That night, I locked the door of the bedroom that Willis and I shared. I didn't want my mother coming in to sit by my side like she sometimes did when she knew I was upset. I didn't want to be comforted.

Our bedroom was so cramped that the heads of our mattresses touched. No way was I going to look at the empty bed next to me, and I sure didn't want to see our two fishing rods crossed together in a corner like a towering X or the pile of schoolbooks and novels Willis had left on the floor—that might send me over the edge. So I covered my face with the blue knit blanket as I lay down, still fully dressed.

But through the loopy weave of the blanket, I could see my brother's banner on the opposite wall. He'd ordered the banner a few years ago from Harvard University, where he planned to go after his high school graduation. I hadn't wanted to think of Willis going away to college, even though that had always been his dream, but now that he'd been arrested, who knew if he was going to even complete his senior year. Everything had changed without any warning, and I didn't know what I hoped for anymore.

I pulled the blanket off my face, sneezed, and looked carefully at the banner. It was decorated with what Willis said was the university's coat of arms, the word *veritas* spelled out in the middle. When I'd asked Willis what a coat of arms was, he had pointed to the triangular shape inside the banner. "Check it out," he'd replied. "See, it's a white shield. A coat of arms protects your identity, who you really are."

I'd wondered then what my identity really was, other than sister to the smartest and coolest person on island, and was glad that my brother was always there to protect me. But that was before.

Later, I'd asked my mother what *veritas* meant. It was a word I'd stared at every day but never thought to wonder about. My mother just shrugged and said she thought it meant something about the truth.

A lone pillow lay on the floor between our beds. The one that Willis always folded in half and stuck behind his head when he read late into the night. I leaned over to pick it up but started to feel dizzy all over again, the way I'd felt after seeing my brother taken to jail. And then the itching began; I didn't need to look down at my chest and arms to know that flame-red hives were beginning to pop up.

I always thought that Willis was pretty perfect and could handle anything that came his way. When he was younger, he'd say that he wanted to be a firefighter when he grew up, someone who rescued children and families from burning buildings. His dream changed when he got to high school and he read some book he really loved. Willis said that the dude in the book wasn't a firefighter but that he rescued people in a different kind of way, although he never really explained how. Not that it made any difference, anyway. Now that Willis was locked up in jail, it would be up to me to do the rescuing. It was right then when I made my birthday vow:

I would get Willis out of jail, no matter what.

CHAPTER THREE

We had pretended for a long time, my mother, Willis, and I. Nobody in my family had the guts to spit out the truth, but we'd all known that something was very wrong. My brother had changed right before our eyes and still we'd acted as if nothing had happened.

It wasn't that Willis had lied outright, but he hadn't told the truth either, and when the truth isn't told, something sticks in the air. Kinda like a cloud ready to burst or an extraterrestrial spaceship of some kind. The ones that hover there, just waiting to explode.

The hovering started slowly, then began to take up more and more room in our island sky.

Maybe my mother had been right that Willis's arrest had been a long time coming. The truth was that my mother and I knew that something was up, although we never spoke to each other about it. Willis had hardly been home anymore, and he seemed more and more distant, rarely ever wanting to wrestle with me on the floor or take me fishing, the way he used to, or even stay up late playing board games, school night or not. He barely answered when we asked him questions. He hardly said anything at all.

Once, he fell asleep at breakfast, his head falling plop into the *Rock Haven Register* newspaper that my mother read each morning. Once, he went to bed right after school, at three o'clock, and wasn't even sick. Twice, he stayed out all night. Soon, he was staying out all night again and again, although my mother begged him not to. When she tried to ground him as a punishment, he just smiled, hugged her, and then spent the whole night out all over again.

"Your brother's having a real hard time," my mother had whispered to me one night, sitting on the edge of my bed. It was very late, and Willis still hadn't come home. "It's tough on a son when his father's not around."

I guess she forgot that it was tough on a daughter too.

But Willis was still my brother and I loved him. I wanted everything to be back the way it used to be and for him to be the same brother I had always known.

I didn't understand it at the time, but as it turned out, none of us would ever be the same.

The first time Willis got arrested was in January, when he and some friends had a party in one of those huge summer mansions on the bluff. It was the dead of winter and the house was all boarded up, but I guess Willis decided it would be fun to see what it was like inside. They sure must have made a lot of noise, Willis and his friends. Guess a neighbor saw them and called the cops.

I'll never forget my mother's face after she got the phone call from the police that night. She wore an expression I'd never seen before: the tight crease of her brow, the sizzle as she shook her head back and forth. The slant of her mouth and the wild green of her eyes.

In April, my brother was arrested again. This time for selling a stolen ring to a friend. I never did find out if it was a diamond ring or just gold, but I guess the friend's parents found it somewhere and knew something was wrong. Seventeen-year-olds don't usually mess around with fancy rings.

This time, my mother's expression wasn't angry, more like alarmed. Watchful, like the way she was when I got really sick and my fever was rising. An invisible net dropped over her whole body, and I could see that she struggled to escape. But she never really did.

Willis wasn't arrested and taken to jail those first two times. My mother had to go to court instead, miss a day of work and wear her frayed pleated skirt, but there were no hand-cuffs, no talk of bail. Once, I overheard something about juvenile detention off island somewhere, but only once.

This time was different.

My brother had been joyriding in someone's car without permission. He'd had a few beers before driving real fast and almost hit a man crossing Ocean Drive. The car went smack into the concrete seawall, and it was lucky that no one was killed.

CHAPTER FOUR

The morning of Willis's joyriding incident, I'd kicked my brother real hard in the shins after he insisted that I should live in Boston instead of Rock Haven since a nickname for Boston is Beantown and my name was Bean. Of course, I knew that he was just teasing, but the idea of not belonging to my island made me mad. Islanders are proud of our home and how we live surrounded by water, separated from the mainland and tough as all get out. But now that Willis had been arrested, I wished I'd never kicked him, Beantown or not.

So why did they call me Bean, anyhow?

I'm really not sure. It had something to do with my size, since I'm not short or tall, but "compact as a fava bean," my mother liked to say. Once, I looked up *fava bean* on the school computer and read that they're "bright green and have a short season." When I mentioned this to my mother, she laughed and patted me on the head. Annoying to say the least.

"Well, you're not bright green, Bean"—she smirked—"and I sure hope that your season isn't a short one." Then she squeezed me hard and swatted my bottom, just like I was some little kid. I grimaced as soon as she turned away. After all, I didn't want to hurt my mother's feelings, but I was definitely too old to be manhandled.

I guess the word *compact* was fair, since I wasn't fat or thin, just built sturdy, different from Willis, whose arms and legs seemed to grow longer each year. Willis never really ran or walked, but loped around with his long legs like some kind of giraffe. His hands were usually stuck in his pockets, his head bent forward as if about to leap ahead. My steps were short, and I had to trot to keep up with him.

I had a round face and straight dirty-blonde hair, long enough to cover my ears, which was a relief since they stuck out like two seashells.

"Nothing noticeable, Bean," my mother always told me when I complained about my ears. "There are many more things to worry about, I can tell you that."

"Beans, beans, good for your heart. The more you eat, the more you fart," Willis used to sing to me when we were small, until I'd grab him by the knees so that he'd trip and fall down. Being short had its advantages.

But now Willis was gone, stuck in the Hancock County jail, probably along with a bunch of hardened criminals. What if they all ganged up and bullied him? What if they planted evidence in his cell so that he'd be blamed for carving a shank out of soap and have to stay there forever? I'd heard about things like that.

So I did what I usually do when I had a problem to solve or just needed a few moments of quiet to myself. The day after my birthday and Willis's arrest, I trudged up the backroads past the lagoon, all the way to the bluff that overlooked Refuge Beach and then up to the rock ledge that curved over the ocean at Lookout Point. As usual, I ignored the yellow-and-red tin sign that said DANGER. DO NOT CLIMB ON ROCKS, since my friends and I had been climbing all over the Point for years and years without ever getting really hurt. It's true that Tommy Costa once broke his arm there, but that was because he got into a fight with his cousin from America, and it really didn't have anything to do with climbing the rocks, just with messing around with his thick-headed cousin who was twice Tommy's size.

The only danger at the Point was that if you ended up there at the wrong time of day, you might run into some teenagers making out, but they most often stayed away during daylight. They'd all meet up just after sunset, like gangs of gross vampires or werewolves, and just have at it, right there in the wide open. You couldn't catch me at the Point at night, no way.

When you first climb down the Point's rocky path, you have to slide over to the right just a few steps, then drop down to the flat ledge where you can see the dark turquoise sea below and straight ahead to the outer arc of land beyond. That's if there wasn't any fog or if it hadn't been raining hard. On this particular day, the sky was clear, the sun was shining, and the ocean below shimmered, edged with navy and pale green just like someone had rolled out two wide silk ribbons. This is how the Rock Haven ocean often looked: blocked with dark and light. The water could be so absolutely calm that it seemed like you could walk right on top.

I sat there by myself on Lookout Point, watching the seagulls complain as they dipped down to the ocean, hunting for fish. The bright colors of green beach grasses, yellow blossoms, and scattered wild dark pink roses all poking up from in between and around the rocks made my eyes smart. I never really figured out how so many different plants and flowers could survive in the island's sand and stone, but come summer, Rock Haven was covered with new growth. Just sandy rock for soil and salt spray for water, but everything kept getting stronger and spreading every single year.

I squatted on the rocky ledge for a few minutes, arms hugging my knees, and feeling the trickle of sweat running down my cheek. It was the end of May, and the weather hadn't gotten real hot yet, but the afternoon sun beat down on my face and shoulders. Weird, no matter what the temperature, when those rays skidded off the water, it felt like you could burn right up right then and there, but then a cool breeze would blow, a cloud would drift, and the moment would pass.

Then I heard Willis's low voice. "Don't sweat it," he'd always say to me. "Don't sweat it, sis." I thought of my mother's sad face and how she'd soon be bagging up chips, soda, and saltwater taffy for the afternoon tourist crowd—the ferry dock was right across the street from Stop & Shop, and after the boat came in was always her busiest time. I thought of my father, far away in some distant town, sleeping in some strange bed, and probably not even knowing what had happened to Willis at my birthday celebration.

Two sailboats floated by below, a white fluttering from the masts. Next, a red kayak on the glistening green-blue water. I shaded my eyes with one hand and made out a large white dog squatting on the kayak's bow, then someone in an orange life jacket, the single oar flipping back and forth from one side to the other. The kayak was going so slowly that it almost looked as if it wasn't moving all, like that red dot would be stuck in the same place forever and ever. Then the ferry's horn and then the ferry itself, chugging into the distant town harbor, the broad top deck crowded with travelers.

It wouldn't be long until the entire island was full to the brim with tourists and summer people, but no matter how many visitors pounded through town from who knows where, in this moment of hot sun, I was completely alone, nobody in the whole world could help me and nobody even knew where I was.

After returning home from the Lookout, I watched my mother make our dinner of macaroni and cheese. It was usually one of my favorites, but once she started talking about Willis, dinner didn't seem all that appealing. My stomach did a few queasy laps when she slowly told me that she'd just gotten word from Sheriff Cobbs that Willis would have to stay in jail for two to three months before sentencing, depending on when a court date was available. Since we probably wouldn't be able to make bail, this was the only option.

The yellow mound of noodles in the bowl quivered as my mother placed it on the table.

"That's dumb. You mean he has to just sit there in jail until the judge gets around to making a decision? That doesn't make sense."

"Bean." My mother said my name as if it was a full sentence. "The facts are the facts and the law is the law." She was still standing by the stove, making herself a cup of tea, so that I was facing her back and could see that she was wearing her brown cardigan sweater inside out over her green uniform, a mistake she often made, the small white neck tag in full view. For a minute she didn't saying anything, and I wanted to reach over and tear off that tag with my own hands.

"We *will* get the bail money, right? We're gonna get Willis out?"

She shook her head again. "It's just too much. The sheriff said that bail is set at a thousand dollars. Where do you think that's going to come from? Do you have any idea how much that actually is?" I could tell my mother was getting angry by the flush creeping up her neck. "And anyway, this is your brother's responsibility and not mine. I have enough on my hands as it is."

But I didn't care one thing about responsibility and whose it might be. Saving Willis from jail was the only thing on my mind, even if I had to do it by myself. Even better, maybe if I talked to my brother, he could help come up with a plan.

"When can we go visit him? He'll know what to do. Can we go visit him tomorrow?"

"I don't have time to go tomorrow," she mumbled. "And you're too young to go by yourself since you're under eighteen."

"So when can we go?"

"Visiting hours are at the same time as my work hours," my mother continued as she unpinned her Stop & Shop badge from her sweater. "I just can't make it all the way over to the jail with you anytime soon. Can't miss any Stop & Shop hours or I won't get my regular check."

I bit my tongue, knowing that sounding off wasn't going to get me anywhere. "Then how come I can't just go alone? Willis is probably waiting for one of us to show, and it would stink if neither of us made it." The thought of my brother expecting our visit made my arms and chest itch furiously.

"Because those are the jail rules. And no matter what your brother believes, rules are made to be followed. Maybe I could take a couple of hours off at the end of next week, but I can't promise anything. There's this new girl in produce who's always late and I have to cover for her."

"But can't you just take off one morning or afternoon?"

"No, I can't. We need the money. You know that."

"We can't leave him there. We have to find money for bail."

"Well, what do you want me to do about it, Bean?" My mother turned around and her face was red. "Life isn't always fair and better that you toughen up now and face the music.

We can't always get what we want, I can sure tell you that. And if the sheriff says you can't visit by yourself, then you cannot visit by yourself. To be honest, I don't much feel like seeing Willis right now, anyway. Too mad and too disappointed."

She finally sat down at the table with her mug of tea and began making her way through her bowl of macaroni in large gulps, her lips smeared yellow. My mother looked like a stranger to me then, hunched over her bowl of food, a strand of hair sticking to one cheek, her brow furrowed, her eyes narrowed, her mouth open wide as she downed every single greasy noodle. I thought of what Willis might be having for his dinner.

"Look, this isn't my fault, is it?" my mother continued in between bites. "Please wipe that unpleasant expression off your face, Bean, and eat your meal."

I didn't care if my expression was unpleasant, so I banged down my fork and stomped right out of the kitchen into my room. I knew that I was being rude. I knew that my mother would probably give me extra chores as a punishment. But that was the least of my problems. So I just lay there on my bed, trying to figure out what to do about Willis. If I didn't come up with a solution quickly, who knows what could happen?

One thousand dollars was a ridiculous number, much more than I'd ever imagined, and there was no way my mother would ever be able to get it. I had ten dollars saved from Christmas last year and a few coins that had dropped behind my bed last week. But that wasn't going to be much of a help. Bail was serious stuff.

I closed my eyes and tried to concentrate. Willis was the one who usually solved problems for both of us. It was kinda scary to be responsible for fixing this one; what if I couldn't figure something out? What would happen to Willis? What would happen to me without him?

The clear, sunny day had turned into a damp, misty evening, and the foghorns started signaling to each other, calling back and forth, back and forth. Willis always complained that the throaty noise kept him up at night, but I found it kind of soothing—two island lighthouses shooting beams from separate cliffs but still connected by sound.

CHAPTER FIVE

I woke up in the morning with one thing on my mind: visiting my brother in jail. Although my mother had said that visitors had to be eighteen or with an adult in order to see prisoners, I figured that the guards might give me some slack. After all, Willis was my very own flesh and blood.

The Hancock County jail was just past town, up the hill, way at the very end of Main Street, something that I always found strange. Wouldn't you think that a professional prison would end up being far away on some dark, winding road at the end of the island instead of a hop and a skip from the center of town?

The island was one place in the summer and another in the winter—kinda hard to wrap your mind around. When you walked down Main Street's narrow sidewalks, this is what you'd see in the store windows from June through August: long, strapless gowns with rhinestone fastenings; antique sofas and chairs that looked too small for real people; or sculptures of ships and paintings of the beach. Who needed paintings when the boats and shore were right there, smack in front of your eyes?

And there were tons of souvenir shops that sold all kinds of stuff, like T-shirts; sweatshirts; wooden maps of the island; plastic, plaster, or paper fish; postcards; seashells; and hats of all kinds, some with little whales or mermaids sewn on the brim. Also a ton of fudge and ice cream shops on every corner.

Rock Haven's tourist trap stores were surrounded by cobblestone streets crammed with white clapboard homes: perfectly landscaped yards and gardens, most of the houses trimmed with black shutters, each looking like a picture from postcards. If only all the tourists knew that they were only steps away from steel bars and the thump of sad hearts.

It took me forever on the L4 and L6 buses to make my way to the jail on Main Street Extension. If I just could have finished repairing my three-speed bike, the trip would have taken half the time, but I still needed to do a bunch of work before I could even think about a short ride. My mother found the bike listed under the Free section in the *Rock Haven Register* a few weeks before my birthday and had walked it all the way home from the Stop & Shop. I thought that was pretty nice of her since it couldn't have been easy to drag the rusty old thing with barely-there tires.

I'd already cleaned the gears with a toothbrush and soap, fixed and reinstalled the crooked front tire, and oiled the chain twice, but I still had to inflate the back tire, which was flat as a pancake. I guess I was pretty good with my hands and enjoyed working outside on warm afternoons, imagining what the bike would look like after I'd finished. I'd even thought about adding some neon handlebar tape and a brand-new horn.

Unfortunately, it still wasn't fixed, and the day I headed out to the jail, it was pouring rain, anyway. The island buses were known to be slow, particularly when the weather was bad. Good thing I'd eaten a light breakfast that morning, because we stopped and started every few minutes, lurching forward and careening to a stomach-churning skid each time anyone on the flooded streets waved us down, including folks with bikes and dogs. This was the deal with the Rock Haven buses, all summer long. You could pick them up at their regular stops or just hail them down anywhere you wanted en route. A waste of time, if you ask me, since it took twice the time to get anywhere, and it wasn't a heap of fun when you're seated next to some funky, wet dog trying to lick your ankles. Dogs weren't my favorite ever since some large, mangy mutt had chased me down Main Street when I was seven.

Lucky that I was wearing my old yellow slicker that morning, even though I'd almost grown out of it, the cuffs too short and the hem barely reaching my waist. Funny how you could grow and grow and not even realize what was happening. It always seemed to me that getting taller should hurt or itch or something so that you knew what was going on in your very own body. One day I was one height and the next another.

The last bus stop was at the edge of town, and I had to make my way on foot for another ten minutes or so in the cold rain. During these kinds of downpours, Rock Haven streets always flooded, and by the time I reached the jail, my jeans were pretty much soaked through and through up to my knees.

So I wasn't in the best of moods when I finally slogged through the jail's front office door.

"Hey, Beano, how you doin'?" Ace Silva called from across the room. Ace had graduated Rock Haven High a few years ahead of Willis, and his younger sister, Yara, and I pretty much hung out all the time ever since we were in the first grade. I knew Ace's real name was Ason, but Willis told me that he'd been teased so much as a kid (for a pretty obvious reason), that he started calling himself Ace.

I nodded hello to the big guy—Ace was tall and definitely wide, and he wasn't exactly a looker. His head was completely bald, making his round face look huge, his snub nose no more than a silly pink blob, and his lips chapped and puffy. And Ace's eyes were lost underneath hooded lids, the whole deal giving him the appearance of an otherworldly creature.

Ace had just been hired as a corrections officer for the jail, an interesting tidbit of information I'd learned from Yara in the spring, and I figured that this would definitely work in my favor. Maybe, because he had just started the job, he wouldn't be up to date on all the jail's visitor rules and regulations. And, anyway, rules were meant to be broken, weren't they?

"Here to make bail for your brother?" Ace guffawed, as if the whole thing was some kind of big joke.

"Well, I don't exactly have the money now," I muttered, trying not to look embarrassed, "but what if I got it later; I mean, what if I got the bail sometime before Willis's sentencing, could I do that? Or do I have to come up with all the money right now?" Ace thought about this for a moment, examining his fingernails as if they were fascinating.

"Sure," he finally said. "Anyone can post bail anytime they want. I hear the judge arraigned him late yesterday afternoon and set bail at one thousand big ones."

I sighed with both relief and disappointment. It was good news that I could bring the bail whenever I got it, but on the other hand, the thought of coming up with one thousand dollars made my teeth hurt. Of course, my mother had already told me the bail amount, but I'd hoped she was wrong. One thousand dollars was a pretty big number. Well, it was an impossible number.

"Thanks." I smiled at Ace, trying to act respectful, although it was hard to think of him as a real guard instead of plain old Ason from high school. "Anyway, I'd like to visit Willis while I'm here." Lucky for me that the sheriff was nowhere in sight.

"Sorry, dude." Ace leaned against the back office wall, pulled out half a mangled sandwich from his pants pocket, and took a monster bite. He reached for the large can of Dr Pepper from his desk and burped. "No can do. Kids have to have an adult with them. Them's the official rules. Come back later with your mom."

I'd just spent almost two hours on two painfully slow buses all the way from the lagoon and then walked in the pouring rain to boot. I wasn't going to come back later. The name Ason sprung to my lips, but I resisted the impulse. It wasn't going to do me any good if I got him angry.

"Come on, Ace. Just for a minute. Promise I won't say anything or tell anyone."

"Nope, no way, José."

Was it my imagination or did Ace look annoyingly pleased with himself as he took the final bite of his disgusting sandwich? It kinda made me squeamish to see him wipe his hands on his creased khaki uniform pants, leaving a long, slimy stain on one leg. "Hey," I finally said, trying to get my anger under control. It seemed ridiculous that my brother was right inside and I couldn't even visit him for a single minute, just to see if he was okay. "Can I leave Willis a note? Can you at least give him a note from me?"

But before Ace had a chance to answer, I heard the shriek of a siren, first faint and then louder and louder.

"Better make yourself scarce, dude," Ace said suddenly, pointing out the window to the parking lot, where a black-and-white cruiser was slowly turning in to a space. "The sheriff doesn't take much to kids hanging around the jail."

So, after shooting Ace the meanest look I could muster, I headed back out the front door, then sprinted around the side of the building before Sheriff Cobbs could catch sight of me. Naturally, it was still pouring rain.

And naturally, it took another full two hours to make my way all the way back to the lagoon.

When I finally got home, soaked to the bone, my mother was already back from work, sitting at the kitchen table, reading the *Rock Haven Register*. She pressed down her index finger on an open page, clearly and rudely indicating that she was otherwise occupied.

"What's up, Bean? You look like you've been through a car wash or something."

I sneezed, brushing wet bangs out of my eyes. "Mom," I said slowly, "I really, really need you to go with me to the jail over the weekend. Just for a quick visit. I've got to talk to Willis before it's too late."

She didn't say anything for a minute and then sighed, her finger still pressed to the newspaper. "Look, Bean, we've already discussed this, and I said loud and clear that I'd let you know when I have the time and energy, but it won't be for a while. And definitely not this weekend. And probably not next either. Now, I really don't want to talk about Willis or jail anymore."

My mother might not have wanted to talk about Willis, but I knew he was on her mind. Even though she didn't want me to see, I could tell that she was as upset as I was. I absolutely knew that. My mother was pretty tough, but she'd definitely changed since the arrest, walking with a new hobble, her back bent just a tad more than usual and her mouth set in a permanent frown.

And so, it was clear that I'd have to be the one to do the rescuing. My mother was just too worn down.

"Seeing Willis won't help anything, anyway," she muttered, almost to herself, turning to look out the kitchen window, where the gray plastic blinds hung sideways, their spines recently cracked. "It is what it is, Bean. It is what it is."

To tell the truth, I was pretty darn sick of hearing that phrase—*It is what it is*—something my mother liked to say when things didn't go her way. I was also tired of being eleven, even though it had only been a few days, since I still couldn't do anything by myself, get a real job, make my own decisions, go see my very own brother in jail. If I could only get the money for bail, Willis would be back home and I wouldn't have to worry about anything.

I'd just have to put my mind to it, tired or not, and figure out some way, any way, to raise the bail cash. It had been three days since my brother's arrest and there would be another thirty to sixty days until his sentencing. We could worry about the sentencing itself later. There was no way I was going to let Willis stay in jail for that long. I may not have always been the sharpest knife in the drawer at school, but I definitely knew how to get things done when I put my mind to it. Except with my mother. She was a different story altogether.

"You can't kid a kidder, little Bean of mine," she'd said to me once when I was trying to con her into one thing or another. "I've got your number, you can be sure of that."

My mother may have thought she had my number, but she didn't have any idea of how far I was willing to go in order to rescue Willis from jail. She didn't know that I was ready to change everything so that things could return to the way they used to be.

CHAPTER SIX

I opened my eyes the next morning, fully dressed and ready for action. Most mornings during the summer, I'd grab my fishing rod and head out to the jetties on Refuge Beach, sometimes stopping to nab some bait from Rusty Thomas's shack on the docks. But on this particular day, I had other plans, and without changing into a fresh T-shirt and jeans or even taking a shower, I bounded into the kitchen and grabbed a cherry Pop-Tart from the cracked yellow Formica counter. Willis had been planning to fix that crack for a good while, but a long piece of soiled adhesive tape remained there instead like a white snake banged flat by someone's fist. I was pretty good with a hammer and nails and a paintbrush too; Willis had taught me how to fix a whole bunch of things, but neither of us ever figured out how to repair that long, winding crack.

My mother had already left for work, so I dashed out the door without having to give any explanation of where I was going. Practically running, I took the main road across from the lagoon toward the bluff, speeding past the thrift store and post office, not even stopping to wave or talk with the kids who called out my name. I wasn't ever the kind of girl who always had a best friend stuck to me like glue. Not that I didn't have friends or wasn't popular or anything—I just liked hanging around with other kids when I felt like it but also hanging with my brother or even by myself. Usually that worked out pretty well.

Most of my friends were off island on vacation, anyway, visiting relatives or out fishing with their families, so the assorted groups of kids hanging out on scratchy yards were either too young or too old to be of any real interest. I heard their thin voices in the wind as I ran ahead.

"Hey, Bean!"

"How's your brother?"

"Wanna go swimming at Horseshoe Beach later today?"

"Bean!"

I kept running, past the bike rental store, where there was a crowd gathered outside; the small diner with a long line snaking all the way into the parking lot; the fish store; the toy store; the pharmacy. Rock Haven's real town center was a couple of miles away, but there were a few assorted restaurants and stores up by the lagoon side of the island.

I sped past the small brick hospital and hung a left at the intersection until I made it all the way to the bluff where the island's largest and fanciest houses lined up like family members in a photograph. Each house had bright trim painted in a jumble of different colors ("That was the style in olden times," Willis had once explained): pink, blue and yellow, green, purple and a mustardy orange, tan, turquoise, violet and peach. When I was just a kid, I thought the bluff mansions were kind of magical, reminding me of my three-layered birthday cakes, little gummy bear families hidden deep inside.

Now that I was older, the mansions just seemed like hulking wastes of space. And all of them had stupid names, as if each deserved special attention just because they were so big. Willis and I would always scoff when we walked past the fancy curlicue signs hanging above the doors: SEA-ESTA, BEACH BLUFF, REEL PARADISE . . . Maybe I should have named my own house: DRIFTWOOD DAD or SINKING SHIP.

But I didn't have time to worry about silly house names or anything else. I needed to concentrate on my recently hatched brainstorm to rescue my brother. I skidded to a stop at Sea-esta, a colossal three-story gray-cedar-shingled mansion with four, count them, four fancy arched porches painted four different mismatched colors, one porch on each side of the front door and another two off a double stained-glass door on the second floor. The entire place was topped off by a widow's walk, a railed narrow walkway on the roof where the story goes that wives used to hang, waiting for their fishermen husbands to return home. For a minute I pictured my own mother nervously pacing up top, on the lookout for my father lost somewhere at sea.

I looked up at Sea-esta, trying to figure out the state of its disrepair. This was my brainstorm; this was how I would get money for Willis's bail. I'd offer my painting and carpentry services to the rich owners and work day and night to wrestle those old houses into shape. Sometimes Willis used to work on mansions over the summer, and although I wasn't officially old enough to be hired, every now and then, he'd let me help him with painting a porch railing or door trim.

Willis taught me how to use long, even strokes with the paintbrush, how to sand down anything the least bit bumpy, and just last summer, he taught me how to nail down loose porch boards so that the floors were steady and strong.

And if Sea-esta's owners didn't hire me, maybe someone else would. After all, the Victorian houses that lined the bluff were often worn, their shingles and porch trim most always battered by wind and salt water, and in need of a quick facelift come the beginning of summer. I was a hard worker. I could whip those old places into shape in no time at all. Well, maybe not in no time, but I was willing to work as much as it took. Quickly, I did the math in my mind:

$10 per hour (I knew that Willis had made $15, but I was six years younger.)

x 8 hours per day = $80 per day

x 7 days a week = $560

x 2 weeks = $1,120

Perfect! If all went my way, I could have Willis's bail money in two short weeks.

I had to admit, though, it made me feel pretty uncomfortable going door to door, asking strangers for work. I knew how dumb I must have looked, an eleven-year-old kid begging to make some cash, although I wasn't exactly begging. It just felt that way, my desperation to help Willis probably written all over my pathetic face.

I tried to look older than I was, standing up straight and tall. But no one even answered Sea-esta's double glass front door. Next I moved on to Ferry Dust, where a woman wearing a white tennis visor said, "No!" before I could even finish my sentence. I knocked on another two bluff houses before anyone else appeared and when they did, the answer was always "How old are you, anyway?" or just plain old no. I guess that most folks weren't all that polite, when you really think about it.

But when I made my way over to Reel Paradise, it was a different story. As I stood at the chipped turquoise front door, a bird suddenly zoomed by my head. Shading my eyes with one hand, I peered at the peeling porch ceiling and noticed a small nest of bluebirds tucked in under one of the porch eaves. It always amazed me how birds knew how to make their homes in the strangest places and build nests out of ordinary things that they picked up as they flew. And it made me feel kinda good that they always seemed to find just the right space to protect their babies. Well, almost.

"You've got guts, child," the old man said, chuckling after he opened the door slowly. He was leaning on a black wooden cane with some kind of carved animal head at the top, his skin reminding me of bark on a tree, so many thin little lines, each connected to one another in tiny triangles. And to my surprise, he was wearing a dark pinstripe suit, despite the warm weather, and a crooked red silk bow tie. It looked as though the old guy was getting ready to go to work in a big city or about to attend a party of some kind.

And his white hair hung down straight around a bald patch at the top of his head, making me think of the frayed shower curtain that circled over Lola Peterson's rusty claw-foot tub. Once, we'd painted one of the tub's porcelain feet with red nail polish, something that got us in a heap of trouble.

"Maybe in a few years," the man wheezed, suddenly waving his cane in front of him as if writing a message in the air. "This tired place surely needs some sprucing up and you might just be the young man to do it in a few years' time. You know, I'm all alone here now in this big house, my wife and children gone. Make sure that you come back when you're older."

A few years? I didn't think so.

I turned away then, without even thanking him. I wasn't a young man and I hated when I was mistaken for a boy, something that happened every once in a while. Just because my hair was short and I didn't dress up shouldn't mean I couldn't be who I really was. And I sure didn't have a few years to wait for a job. I needed the money right then and there.

But the old man called me back, insisting on shaking my hand, his skin dry and papery, and then closed the door behind him slowly, leaving me feeling pretty discouraged. Yet, giving up wasn't an option and there were still a few other houses left that I hadn't yet tried. Just as I sighed heavily, preparing myself for yet another rude no, I heard a high-pitched voice call out from behind me:

"Hey, you, look it, look it, look it, I think I see a skunk! Come see!"

I turned around slowly. Skunks were common on the island, but they usually slept under houses all day, showing up only at night. Why would I want to see a skunk, anyway? Who in her right mind would risk getting sprayed? It wasn't exactly a pleasant scent. I sighed. Standing a few steps behind me was a little girl with curly brown hair; it was hard to tell her age, but she definitely looked younger than me.

"Phoebe," she said, reading my mind. "My name's Phoebe D. Sinclair and I'm nine and I live over there."

Phoebe D. Sinclair? Give me a break. And the girl didn't look anywhere near nine.

My first thought was to ignore her and continue knocking on mansion doors, offering my services. Then a shiver of pleasure ran through me. *Wait*, I thought to myself. *This could be good.*

"You live here in this house?" Anchors Away loomed in front of me, just waiting to be sanded, scraped, and painted.

"Nope, not here. Over there."

I looked over to where the girl was pointing one door down: Beach Bluff, a rambling house with a wide front door painted lavender, and dark green flower boxes bursting with light blue hydrangeas and white lilies of the valley at every oversized window. Naturally, it had a long, welcoming porch wrapped around the front with two oversized white wicker rocking chairs and a round wicker table to match. The house was shingled, like every other house on the bluff, except for a triangle of white siding in the shape of fish scales that filled the space between the top floor and roof eaves. I squinted and looked higher; there was an even smaller tower reaching up to the sky reminding me of the fairy tales I'd read as a kid about a castle and princesses. It seemed to me that most kid books have some kind of trapped princess, locked up and in need of being saved.

Phoebe D. Sinclair's house was actually the very largest one on the bluff, and I could see from where I was standing that it was also more colorful than most, but that its pastel trim colors were definitely faded and peeling. A rusted, old-fashioned iron mailbox hung at a lopsided angle by the wide front door and a tangle of overgrown vines twisted up and around the peeling porch columns. Maybe I could add gardening to my list of employable activities.

"Wanna meet my pup?" Phoebe's voice startled me. "She's learning how to guard our house. She eats scrambled eggs and tofu for breakfast. But she likes blueberries and cranberry juice best. Want to meet her?"

I hesitated. Scrambled eggs and tofu? Blueberries and cranberry juice? But Phoebe could be just the break I needed, if I wanted an in painting houses. I didn't like dogs, but a little puppy couldn't pose much danger, could it?

"Well?" The girl started tapping one foot impatiently.

I resisted the urge to knock off her tapping with a swift kick. Instead, I turned to look down into her questioning face. It was then that I saw that she probably was about nine after all, despite her height. Something about the look in her eyes gave her age away—kind of a sad, weary sort of look. She looked like a kid and still not a kid.

Phoebe had a spray of freckles spread across a snub nose and dark gray eyes tipped downward at the corners like cherry stems. Her eyebrows were brown, knitted together over her nose, and her cheeks were sunken. She was very, very thin. Her shoulder-length curly hair flew around her head like a crowd of wild birds, and she had on a light blue floaty dress over white shorts and a sleeveless pink top. A double strand of red-and-yellow beads swung around her neck, clattering together each time she moved. I also saw that her feet were completely bare, and her toes painted with chipped purple nail polish. She looked ridiculous.

"Sure," I replied slowly, carefully trying to keep my distance. "Sure, I'd like to meet your puppy."

"My nanny says you have to tell me your name first. Kind of silly, I know, but that's the rule. Can't talk to anyone without a name."

A nanny? She had to be kidding.

"Bean," I finally answered. "My name is Bean Wright. Any chance that your parents are home? I have something real important to ask them."

CHAPTER SEVEN

A pup?

If I hadn't known better, I might have thought the pale gray creature spread out on the other side of Beach Bluff's gate was a beached baby whale—gigantic swollen belly shuddering with each wheezy breath.

I glanced over at Phoebe, who didn't seem in the least concerned about the death trap we could be facing. She was trying to grab my hand to pull me closer to her guard dog, something I wasn't having any part of.

I gulped and took a step back.

It lay there on Beach Bluff's front walkway, its gigantic head probably the size of two basketballs, torso almost covering the entire sandy walk. And its jowls, at first unrecognizable, stretched out flat on the ground, oozing with a thick layer of foam underneath and lying on either side of the dog's face like supersized pancakes. The tip of a bright pink tongue stuck out from its black muzzle. A dark, wet nose twitched every few seconds, its shape like a shrunken anchor, curling down on each side above the deep nostrils, then curved up like a comma below. Most startling was the deeply collapsed brow, rows and rows of folds covering its eyes and making me wonder how in the world it could even see.

And I'd never seen a dog that was quite the color of this brute. Silver with tints of dark, almost blackish-blue short fur, the top of its head light and the jowls deepening to a surprising purplish gray. Its fur was short and faded from one shade to the next. Dark paws, jaws, and tail. Light legs, body, and head. Except for the stomach, which I couldn't see much of.

Believe me, I had no problem with that.

"Aren't guard dogs supposed to bark or something?" I whispered to Phoebe. But she just shook her head and started to chomp on her fingernails like she was demolishing a piece of corn on the cob. I made a mental note never to touch that particular hand.

The only thing separating the two of us from possible danger was the house's wobbly front gate, held shut by who knows what.

A low rumble. Was it my imagination or did the ground under my feet tremble? In an embarrassing moment of weakness, I clutched at Phoebe's skinny arm, despite myself.

"Look," she said, grinning and pointing, "she's waking up!"

And then to my surprise and horror, the gigantic animal shook its bloated basketball head, sniffed the air as if hunting for prey, then slowly, very slowly, sighed. Its entire body heaved, then rolled to the other side. To my disgust, its paws, covered with sprouts of black fur like a Dr. Seuss creature's hairy ankles, were as big as my brother's hands, the nails long and thick.

Dog or monster?

Holy moly, I thought to myself. *Holy moly*.

But that was that. To my surprise and relief, once the animal turned over to its other enormous side, it simply went back to sleep, long tail thumping on the ground for a minute, then curling under one hind leg. Its whole body quivered, letting out the sound of a balloon losing air.

Then an unfamiliar smell, kind of fishy, kind of mildewy. I coughed. Phoebe laughed and pointed.

"Phew," she giggled. The dog was completely still. I took a deep breath, then quickly regretted it.

"It's not sick, is it? That dog doesn't look too good." My voice sounded weak and trembly. It seemed that something with the animal wasn't quite right and I had heard that dogs with rabies were to be avoided at all costs. One bite and it was all over.

"Nah," Phoebe said cheerfully. "She farts all the time. Want me to wake her up again?"

"No! Let's just let it sleep for a while. It probably needs a nap."

"Hey!" Her voice was so loud that it made me nervous. I was certain that the beast might wake up again at any minute. I stumbled backward a few more steps for safety. "Beanie, wanna hear me count in Italian? Edwin taught me how to count and some other words too. I can say *please, thank you,* and *good evening*."

Edwin? I didn't even bother to ask.

"Shh." I motioned to the animal, covering my lips with one finger. "Let's not wake up your dog. And my name isn't Beanie. It's Bean. Can't you remember that?"

Phoebe stopped hopping and looked up at me, one grimy hand over her right eye. "If I do this, if I cover my eye with this hand, it looks like there's two of you. Weird. Kinda weird."

"Fascinating," I muttered under my breath, scratching the spreading hives under my shirt. Now that I'd gotten Phoebe to show me her house, I was planning how to ditch her, once I'd convinced her parents to give me work. The last thing I needed was some pipsqueak following me around everywhere. But, then again, there was still the problem of the guard dog. How in the world was I going make it up Beach Bluff's front steps with a thousand-pound beast watching over the property? It wouldn't sleep forever, would it?

Clearly Phoebe was determined to frighten me more, because she spun around, nudged open the front gate with a smidgen of a hand, and actually skipped over to the dog's impossibly long tail. "Hiya, puppy!" she bellowed, pulling on the creature's right ear with all her might. "Wake up, why don't you. Time to wake up and play, why don't ya!"

I was so close to the back edge of the sidewalk by then, I found myself stumbling right into the street. I frantically looked one way and then the other for possible assistance, in case of an emergency. The packs of tourists, usually crowding the road on their rented bikes, were nowhere to be seen. Who would come to my rescue if the dog monster woke up and decided that it didn't like strangers? After all, Phoebe certainly wouldn't be any help.

"Come on in, Beanie," Phoebe called to me from behind the gate. To my horror, she was actually bouncing one foot up and down on the monster's quivering belly. "Come meet my dog. Come on in and meet Honey Sinclair."

CHAPTER EIGHT

When Phoebe introduced Edwin as her nanny, I was shocked.

Hardly my vision of a plump, grandmotherly type with an apron, cheeks dusted with baking flour.

Phoebe's nanny was a he, not a she, and was walking out Beach Bluff's door toward us, wearing a white button-down shirt that bulged open every inch or so, revealing wisps of straggly red chest and belly hair that made me want to heave. Wrinkled khaki shorts belted under an extra-large paunch, the belly flopping over his waist like a recently caught halibut, and some kind of tattered, grayish fleece slippers, a strange choice for a summer outfit. His red hair was thinning at the crown, the rest swept in an oily-looking mound at the back of his head; I had the sudden urge to find a pair of scissors and hack it right off. I'd never seen a man with a bun before, although a few of the hippie wash-ashores on island wore sloppy ponytails, something my mother never approved of.

So this was Edwin, and he was not exactly what I'd call cheerful caregiver material. His mouth was set in a sour grimace and copper-colored, caterpillar-shaped eyebrows met together over a wide nose. He had small brown eyes that blinked so fast I thought he might just need a pair of heavy-duty glasses. Also a wobbly double chin with a bristle of red beard and one earring sunk in a fleshy lobe. Although the guy's stomach was impressive, his arms and legs looked kinda scrawny.

This was definitely not someone I'd ever want to be my personal caretaker, or even acquaintance for that matter. Willis or no Willis.

Edwin looked down at me from the front porch, blinking like crazy, and when he smiled a slight, tight-lipped kind of smile, I smiled back. But this redheaded, non-grandmotherly, non-nanny nanny made me feel kinda shy, something pretty unusual for me. Maybe it was because when Edwin looked at me, his eyes seemed to slice open my entire face, uncovering something inside me that I was trying to hide. And when he made his way down the weedy brick walkway toward us, a big yellow bowl in hand, I resisted the urge to run the other way.

Edwin set the bowl down next to Honey, then looked up as Phoebe introduced me as her new neighbor. Neighbor? Hardly. I was a lagoon kid, not a bluff kid. The nanny shook my hand; his handshake was gentle but firm.

"Can we please bring Honey inside, Edwin?" Phoebe whined, hugging the big dog tightly. "Just for today?"

"You know the rules, Phoebe," Edwin said with a frown. "The dog stays outside in the front yard during the day."

"Edwin's from Sydney, Australia. Down Under," Phoebe announced, pulling at my arm after he went back inside the house. "And he's really pretty okay, once you get to know him, although really strict. He's a chef and kinda old, but Mother thought he'd be perfect for me since he knows how to cook gourmet and came highly recommended by another family with kids. I love gourmet, don't you?" She was quiet for a minute as if considering the possibilities of meals to come. "Come on, Beanie, hurry up. Let's get some cookies. They're in the kitchen."

Phoebe's nanny hadn't sounded foreign to me, and he also hadn't looked like any gourmet chef, but it really wasn't my business, anyway. I had bigger fish to fry, after all, and finding myself inside one of the bluff's enormous houses boded well. This was my very first time to be invited into a real island Victorian mansion, even after living in Rock Haven my whole entire life. But just like Phoebe's nanny, the old place wasn't exactly what I imagined or expected. I guess it was just the day for strange surprises.

First of all, it was dark inside Beach Bluff, despite all the large windows, since they were covered by thick curtains, every last one. And there was something almost eerie about the way the morning light spilled in underneath those heavy brown window drapes, windows every which way you looked. Straight up and down windows, square, short windows, and arched windows that reminded me of the church down by the island elementary school. So many windows, all smothered by heavy folds of curtains, even though it was the middle of the day. And the little light that managed to sneak in had specks of smoky glitter, a dusty sparkle that seemed too thick to breathe, making you feel like you might just choke. When I started to follow Edwin and Phoebe down the corridor toward the kitchen, I began to feel strange, wobbly, out of sorts, kind of dizzy. Just like on my birthday, when Willis was taken away.

Vertigo.

I felt hot, then cold.

Everything turned blurry.

Beach Bluff's dark wooden floor lurched one way and then another; I was sliding down under.

I saw Edwin at the other end of the hallway. He turned around slowly, very slowly, as if he knew something was wrong but wasn't sure he wanted to be bothered. His face shrank, then expanded, then shrank again. Phoebe was a faint puff of ghostly tulle in the far distance.

"Willis," I whispered, without knowing why. "Willis is gone."

And then the dusty, smoke-glittery hallway went all white. Everything went white, white as island snow, white as my mother's face on my birthday night, white as a blank piece of paper, the kind you always mean to write something important on but never actually do.

When I opened my eyes again, I was lying on a narrow, rust-colored velvet couch in an enormous room, Phoebe pulling on my arm. My head was aching, and my mouth felt dry.

"EDWIN, SHE'S AWAKE!!" Phoebe's sharp voice startled

me, and I tried to sit up, but she pushed me back down with one hand. I guess I was still pretty weak. Before I knew what was what, Edwin appeared from nowhere and handed me a tray with a tall glass of water and a tiny orange neatly arranged in between two white flowers. I looked at the flowers suspiciously. Was I supposed to eat them along with the silly-looking orange? I'd never seen an orange so small.

"I want one too," Phoebe called as Edwin turned away. "You know that they're my favorite!" Phoebe frowned down at me, poking at my shrunken piece of fruit with her pinkie.

Edwin came back quickly with another tray for Phoebe. He looked down at me and grimaced. "Low blood sugar," he murmured. "Best to eat something now if you want to feel better again."

Weren't folks from Australia supposed to have some kind of accent? I was pretty sure that the Australian standing above me sounded like most everyone else I knew. While he didn't speak with the distinct clip of islanders, he sure didn't sound all that different from other wash-ashores.

Strange. Something was fishy.

Phoebe and I sat together on the velvet couch, the material feeling stiff against my arms and not the least bit velvety. I stared at the wall across from me, trying to make out shapes from the patterns of flaking paint. The house was fancy and yet not fancy at the same time and in serious need of a paint job. Kinda surprising to see a mansion so run-down. But who was I to judge? And more work for me, anyway, painter and carpenter extraordinaire!

I watched Phoebe carefully peel away the thin rind, neither of us saying anything. She popped two sections into her mouth with a satisfied grin and then impatiently reached over to my plate in order to help me tear away the bitter skin of what turned out to be the most delicious miniature orange in the entire world.

So why, after I gobbled it up, juice dribbling down my chin, did I have the peculiar thought that I might have just eaten something I shouldn't have, something tainted by the mysterious nanny. After all, *Down Under* sounded suspiciously creepy, even though I knew my imagination was getting the best of me. It was a thought that vanished as soon as it came, but the sharply sweet taste of that unusual orange hung in my mouth for the rest of the day, a reminder that all might not be right in Phoebe's old mansion, the dark and rambling Beach Bluff.

PART TWO

VOICES

CHAPTER NINE

Strange how you grow up with some ideas stuck in your head. Before meeting Phoebe, I'd never really thought of families from the bluff as real people but more like figments of my imagination, characters from books, instead of ordinary flesh-and-blood humans. Don't get me wrong, I wasn't completely out of my mind and didn't think they were aliens or something, but the lives of those folks seemed so distant from mine that I just assumed that they were too different to ever get to know.

My brother and I never hung out with anyone other than friends on the lagoon side of the island, and I somehow understood that my mother might worry if she knew I'd been spending so much time with folks from a bluff mansion, not because I wouldn't like them, but because they wouldn't like me. As if our family wasn't good enough, although that was something she'd never admit. So I just kept my mouth shut about Phoebe, Edwin, Honey, and Beach Bluff. Better to say nothing.

Because despite my disturbing morning at the old house the day before, I still was as determined as ever to get on with my plan to earn money for the bail. I hadn't had the chance to bring the subject up to Phoebe yesterday, so I made my second visit to Beach Bluff first thing the next day.

After all, Willis didn't have all the time in the world. Just the thought of him, alone and locked up, made a line of hives on my neck rise up and take notice.

Phoebe and the hulking Honey greeted me at Beach Bluff's front gate, and both looked up for a second as I approached. Neither seemed the least bit interested in giving me a second glance, so I just stood there for a minute, feeling kinda foolish. Phoebe was busy feeding blueberries to her mess of a supersized animal, her skinny fingers stained dark blue, and each time she gave a fistful of berries to the dog monster, she popped another bunch in her own mouth.

"Why should we hire you to paint our house?" Phoebe asked me when I finally presented my idea to her. "You're just a kid and not even a real painter, Beanie." Then, adding to my humiliation, Phoebe turned to Honey and began to talk directly to the dog, as if I wasn't standing there right in front of her.

And it was Bean, not Beanie.

"First of all, Beanie's not even a grown-up, Honey, and she doesn't have very good manners, anyway. I think Beanie should say good morning to you, and second of all, well, I might not really have a second of all, but her painting the house sounds like a stupid, stupid idea."

Stupid idea? I'd show her stupid. She was arranging a pink silk bow on top of Honey's chunky head, trying to steady it with one hand. Every time the dog breathed, the bow would slide off, landing on a damp, disgusting, deeply creased jowl. Stupid idea? Who talks to a dog, anyway?

"It's not your decision," I replied, eyeing Phoebe's triple strand of fake rhinestones and her lopsided tissue paper crown. The outfit of the day included striped pink-and-white leggings, finished off with some kind of loose yellow lace dress that looked three sizes too big and that dipped below her knees. "I wasn't asking for your permission, just for you to talk to your parents. It sure looks as though Beach Bluff could use some touching up."

To say the least. The old place was peeling away right and left. But I was eager to stay on Phoebe's good side and didn't want to risk getting her mad.

"Hmm . . ." She took the tiara off her head and tried to attach it over Honey's floppy, triple-sized ears. The beast barely moved. "Too small. Honey, I've got to get you a bigger crown, but don't worry, I bet I can find a pretty one for you in town. And we'll get you some more cranberry juice too." She looked up at me brightly. "Phoebe just adores cold cranberry juice, but she's only allowed to drink a little bit at a time or she might get a bellyache."

For a minute, I thought about giving up. Phoebe definitely was going to be a challenge, and I wasn't about to stand there forever as she chattered on and on to a sluggish hunk of animal. I doubted if the dog really even had a pulse.

Phoebe looked up at me with a sudden, eager grin. "Hey, want to help me dress her up real fancy today? Maybe a ruffled skirt and matching hat."

I sighed. I tried to keep the image of my brother in my mind. I tried to hold my temper and not tell Phoebe that she was an idiot.

"Phoebe," I said slowly and evenly, "did you hear what I said about painting your house? Do you think you could please ask your parents? I really need a job."

"Oh, okay." She popped up quickly, leaving the bow and tiara on the ground, and I watched Honey's humongous pink tongue emerge from her gigantic jaws. She licked the ribbon quickly, then crunched the tiara with a single bite. One minute it was there, the next minute, it was gone. Talk about hungry.

I took two steps backward and clutched one of the fence's sharp pickets. You never knew when a weapon might come in handy.

"Come on, Beanie. What are you waiting for?"

Once again, I followed Phoebe up the old house's front steps, having first, just like the day before, made a careful circle around Honey. Phoebe didn't seem in the least bothered that her tiara had become lunch and skipped up Beach Bluff's front steps, apparently not having a care in the world. Her ratty mess of curls was tied in two pigtails with what looked like ragged rope, and they bounced up and down as she screeched, "EDWIN! EDWIN! WHERE ARE YOU? Time's a wastin' . . . EDWIN!"

"Time's a wastin'"?! Where did the kid learn that stuff?

Edwin didn't look the least pleased when he opened the front door. He stood on the front porch for a minute, hands on his hips, before quietly and slowly saying, "Yes, Phoebe?"

I was surprised to see that Phoebe's nanny was wearing more appropriate clothes, a blue apron tied tightly around his large waist with the words *Kiss the Cook* spelled out in silver letters. My arms broke out in goose bumps. Just the thought of kissing this particular cook made me want to hurl.

"What are you making, Edwin?" Phoebe seemed delighted at the sight of the apron. "Your special spaghetti and meatballs?"

"Yes, as you wish." Edwin brushed his forehead with one hand, evidently exhausted by his workload. "Whole wheat pasta and red sauce. Parmigiano Reggiano on top. Now what can I do for you? My water's about to boil."

CHAPTER TEN

Edwin said I could most definitely *not* paint Beach Bluff and that the idea was *ridiculous*, seeing that I was just a *child* and that he didn't *have the authority* to let me *do so*, anyway. He agreed that the old house was in disrepair, but Phoebe's parents only rented it for the summer, and they were the only ones able to get in touch with the landlord, *should they wish to hire a full-grown adult*. Since they were in Europe, *that wasn't likely*.

So Phoebe's parents weren't even on island and certainly not sipping cocktails on the back porch, as I'd imagined, but actually gallivanting around Europe, leaving their daughter behind.

Edwin communicated this information to me slowly and carefully, as if each word was a big effort, and then quickly exited the porch back into the house wearing his silly fleece slippers.

Just like that.

Phoebe and I sat on Beach Bluff's front porch, watching Honey—luckily, a safe distance away—as she heaved up and down in her sleep. A flutter of panic rose in my chest, and I could feel my heart racing faster and faster. What was I going to do?

The thought of going from bluff house to bluff house again, begging for work, was pretty horrible, and probably useless too. Maybe Phoebe was right, after all; who would really hire an eleven-year-old girl to paint their beach mansion when there were adult professionals around? What had I been thinking?

But if not that, what?

"You know, Beanie," Phoebe's voice interrupted my thoughts, "I kinda wish I had a little pretty fluffy white dog instead of a great big one like Honey, a puppy I could carry around and sleep with every night. Honey doesn't do any tricks or even move much at all. And I have to feed her all the time because she's always hungry, hungry, hungry. I wish I had a cute dog who did funny tricks and didn't eat all the time."

"How long have you had Honey?" Not that I was really interested.

"Just a week and a few days. Since Edwin and I got here for the summer. My parents had her sent over to us from the breeder by special airplane. They thought we needed a guard dog to keep us safe." Phoebe giggled. "Glad that airplane didn't crash down from the sky since Honey's so big!"

Although the ferry was the means of transportation to Rock Haven for most folks, the island did have a little airport, where small planes could land and take off. "Only for the rich," my mother used to grumble. "Waste of space and good money, if you ask me." But the image of Honey crammed into one of those little planes was actually pretty funny, and I couldn't help letting out a chortle. Just imagining her big butt squeezed in a narrow passenger seat made me forget about Willis for a moment.

"You know, Honey's worth a whole bunch of money," Phoebe said happily. "She has really famous parents. She's Italian and has fancy papers and won a big prize in the ring."

I may have let out another snort of laughter, this one louder. "Sure, that's if you sell her by the pound." Phoebe looked confused.

"No," she announced, clearly a tad irritated. "All of her. My parents bought all of her for a ton of money. We even got a stamped piece of paper with her blood on it."

"Blood?"

"Yeah, her blood and her mom and dad's blood too. And their mom and dad's." Phoebe was standing up now, in order to emphasize her point.

"Bloodlines. You mean bloodlines, Phoebe." A cold breeze wafted over me, and a familiar voice interrupted Phoebe's announcement.

Edwin was standing right behind us. Amazing how the guy could just sneak up on you without making a sound. Maybe that was the point of the ugly fleece slippers. "Your dog is an Italian Neapolitan mastiff and has excellent bloodlines. Mastiffs are known for being brave and excellent fighters throughout history and their ancestors once fought lions in ancient Rome. Your parents have papers noting her bloodlines. Now it's time for lunch. Will your friend be joining us, Phoebe?"

"And she cost a whole bunch, right, Edwin, right? Millions

and millions of dollars?" Phoebe seemed more interested in how much Honey cost than my joining her for lunch, and I wasn't really sure about going back inside Beach Bluff, anyway, unless I was getting paid, considering my last disastrous experience.

"It's impolite to discuss money." Edwin looked displeased, but he was a generally grumpy kind of guy, so it was hard to tell. "But Honey is descended from an important line of show dogs and is worth about three thousand dollars. Hardly millions, Phoebe. Let's not exaggerate. Now come inside and wash your hands before the pasta becomes overdone."

Three thousand dollars? Had I heard Edwin correctly? Three thousand dollars for that heap of fat, gristle, and bones?

"Want to come in for lunch, Beanie?" Phoebe was already pulling on my arm. "Come on, let's get some lunch and then we can dress up Honey in some of Mother's clothes. She had a bunch shipped over in trunks."

I was pretty hungry by then and let Phoebe lead me through Beach Bluff's front door, despite serious reservations, but dressing up Honey wasn't on my mind. Another plan for the dog was already hatching in my brain, and if letting Edwin feed me could be a step toward accomplishing that plan, I was all in.

My lunch with Phoebe that day began what was to become a daily event for a while. It wasn't that I didn't have anything better to do, but I was absolutely determined to pull off my newly inspired plan to get cash for Willis. And Phoebe was an important part of whether or not I'd be successful. But I would have to play my cards right.

What was my plan?

It was brilliant. It was spectacular. It would solve everything! My plan was to get Phoebe to sell Honey.

The big dog was worth three thousand dollars, an amount of money I could hardly even imagine! And my plan wasn't only a selfish one; I'd use the money from Honey's sale to help Phoebe buy the exact little puppy she wanted while also using some for Willis's bail. And if there was any cash left over, I'd give it all to Phoebe. Honey was her dog and it wouldn't be fair if I kept any extra money for myself. But I felt pretty okay about taking what I needed to rescue my brother, even though I knew it wasn't really exactly right. Sometimes, what was right wasn't always what was best.

Each morning, for the next week, and after a quick mouthful of breakfast at home, I'd head over to the bluff and spend some time trying to get on Phoebe's good side. It wasn't always what I felt like doing, but it was absolutely necessary in order to pull off my new plan and get my hands on bail money. After all, the kid might not go for my idea unless I got her to like and trust me.

Sometimes, we'd take a short walk halfway to town, as far as Phoebe was allowed without Edwin's supervision. Sometimes, I'd show her how to make rock sculptures by piling stones on top of one another into all kinds of different shapes; sometimes, I'd point out all the ducks sliding across the shallow ocean water; sometimes, we'd just sit on her porch and talk, and sometimes—and these were pretty miserable times for me—we'd experiment dressing up Honey in one of Phoebe's mother's hats, scarves, or even oversized, billowy silk shirts, but those were always a pretty tight squeeze.

Believe me, I didn't exactly enjoy any of this—it was perfect fishing weather, and I could have been standing in the sun at the end of one of Refuge Beach's jetties, casting my line and waiting for the thrill of a bite. But I had to think of spending time with Phoebe as a kind of investment. After all, if this brilliant plan was going to work, the kid would have to really like me.

I knew what I was doing was kinda sleazy, and sometimes I even felt a tad guilty as I cozied up to Phoebe by complimenting her weirdo outfits or encouraging her to talk about wanting a new puppy. We'd sit together on the sandy ground, making Honey look as silly as possible in fancy hats or weaving her garlands out of wild beach roses.

"It's not fair that I can't even take her for a walk," Phoebe often complained, staring at the big animal and sighing deeply as if this was the end of the world. "Edwin said that she's too big for me to take out alone, and he has to do it even though he hates, hates, hates walking Honey. Sometimes I sure wish I had a nice little dog that I could take for a walk on a pretty bedazzled leash, or even carry in a basket, you know, the way they do in those movies and in magazines. I could buy a sweet little basket and take the puppy everywhere I went."

"I know," I'd agree quickly. "Really a pain to have such a big dog since you can't do anything with her. And a sweet, cute puppy would be so much fun. Just think how easy it would be to dress up!"

I'd keep a fake smile plastered over my face when Phoebe chattered about carrying a dog in a basket. I'd nod sympathetically, all the time thinking that hauling a puppy around in a basket sounded pretty silly, and then I'd make up all kinds of stories about small dogs, giving them heroic capabilities and perfumed, perfectly groomed locks. Most of my teachers at school said my spelling was subpar but that I could write an okay paper. A for creativity and C for spelling and organization.

One of the stories I made up for Phoebe included a Maltese named Helen of Troy, a blonde, blue-eyed bombshell of a miniature dog with long, wavy curls that had special powers of strength and that saved me from drowning in a terrible riptide at Hermit Beach.

Phoebe was skeptical, to say the least. "What's a riptide and how could such a little dog rescue a whole entire person?"

I could see that I may have gone too far with my story. "A riptide is when there's this real strong current where you could drown. And if no one's around to save you, or you don't know the right way to swim around it, well, then you just might go under."

"But I still don't see how such a small dog could save you.

That doesn't make any sense. Did she pull you by your bathing suit straps?"

"Yes," I said quickly, blushing a bit. It did sound pretty silly when I thought about it again. "Yes, exactly. I was wearing one of those bathing suits that tied around my neck, so Helen just chomped down on the knot and pulled me with her teeth. Of course, I kicked my legs to help her and wasn't really that far from shore."

"But where is Helen of Troy now?" Phoebe asked me, still clearly unconvinced. "And why did you name her that? Was it after Zeus's daughter? Does she still live with you and your family?"

I couldn't exactly remember who Zeus and Helen of Troy were, although I knew they both had something to do with the Greeks. We studied the Greeks in school last year, but I hadn't been, as usual, really concentrating. I knew I'd have to think quickly.

"No." I shook my head sadly. "No, we had to send Helen off island. That's where all the hero dogs go, you know, all the dogs who do good things."

"Aren't the hero dogs lonely? Don't they miss their friends and families?"

I could see that I was going downhill quick and needed to think fast.

"Oh, no, they're treated really well. The president wants them to live in luxury, so they all stay together in a fancy dog castle." Who was I kidding. Fancy dog castle?!

"What president?"

"You know, the president-president. The president of the United States. He takes an interest in animal things, all of the United States of America's important animal policies and laws. In fact, I just read that he passed a new bill."

Phoebe considered this for a moment. I might have pushed my luck with the president stuff; after all, Phoebe wasn't an idiot and could be pretty sharp at times. I held my breath.

"Well," she finally said, "I guess it's okay that you had to send her to the dog castle because I bet she gets all kinds of nice things there."

"Definitely." I nodded eagerly. "The president makes sure that those dogs get whatever they want, including gourmet dog food. Also cranberry juice, blueberries, or just about anything. It's all paid for by real estate taxes, so it doesn't cost the American people a cent."

I wasn't exactly sure what real estate taxes were but thought it sounded pretty official.

"Not cranberry juice and blueberries." Phoebe was eyeing me suspiciously. "I bet you're making that up because you know that they're Honey's favorite. I'm not stupid, you know."

"I was just teasing you about that part!" Luckily, I was quick to come up with a cover.

Thank goodness Phoebe was only nine. One year older and I might have been in deep trouble.

CHAPTER ELEVEN

When you're just a little kid, you never think of making friends with people who are different from you. You just figure that they'd speak another language or something. Why bother to get to know someone whose life has nothing to do with yours? There probably wouldn't be any way to get along or even understand each other. That's how us lagoon kids felt about the bluff families. I think that's how our parents felt too.

But to my surprise, after a while, that really wasn't the deal with Phoebe, or at least, it didn't seem to be. She sure did live differently from me or anyone else I knew, yet, when you took away her house and nanny, she was almost regular underneath. Sure, the kid dressed up like a nutjob and probably couldn't swing a hammer, cast a fishing rod line, or skip a rock in a pond the way I could, but all in all, she was okay.

But that's not to say I actually liked her.

She sure could be annoying.

And still, there was something about Phoebe that sometimes made me sad.

She told me that her parents had just hired Edwin right before they left on their European vacation in May. He would take care of her until their return mid-June. An entire month seemed to me to be a very long time to be away from your own kid. Especially hiring a new nanny just before leaving the country—that couldn't be a good idea. Edwin was a perfect example of a plan gone bad.

But Phoebe didn't seem the least bit disturbed by any of it. Apparently, she was used to having new nannies. "They mostly don't stay more than year at a time," she told me, "and it's important not to get too attached or you'll feel bad after they leave. Once, I had a really mean nanny who wouldn't let me dress the way I liked but she didn't stay long. And Mother says it really doesn't matter if the nannies are all that nice to me, anyway, because Mother and Father are plenty nice enough."

I looked at her hard for a minute, to see if she was joking, but she just smiled her funny, lopsided little Phoebe smile and changed the subject to wishing she had a little sister. "That way," she explained, "I wouldn't be alone so much of the time and would always have someone to play with."

"I have an older brother," I said suddenly, surprised as the words slipped out of my mouth. "But he's away right now."

"A brother?" Phoebe seemed to brighten at the thought. "I wish I had a brother. Where is he? How long will he be away?" I shrugged, hesitant to say any more.

"Learning how to be a firefighter," I replied, my head down. "He's away at firefighting school and won't be back for a while."

• • •

Like most of the house, Phoebe's bedroom was dark, the large windows covered by thick curtains, lined with silk tassels at the bottom, reminding me of the graduation cap Willis might never get to wear. Completely bare walls, with the exception of a faded, wood-framed embroidery of a cottage with the words *Sleep, Little Child* written underneath. The stitched steps to the cottage and its front door had worn off so that it looked like the small house was floating in space with no way for those inside to get out.

"My room at home in Providence is different," Phoebe told me one day. "It has pretty yellow wallpaper with a blue flower border, but I like this one too."

Phoebe loved books, and she had quite a collection in piles all over the floor. I picked up one with a fancy cover of some girl in pigtails hanging out on a mountainside with two old men shepherds and a bunch of goats: *Heidi*. I opened the book and leafed through it quickly. Not exactly my cup of tea.

Phoebe also loved small things, trinkets of all kinds. Her pockets were usually filled with little stones gathered from the front yard or from the bluff beach beyond. She also collected miniature pine cones, tiny seashells, bits of sea glass, and even tidbits of sand. Her bedroom in Beach Bluff was full of it all: flowered saucers crammed with small treasures found outside or brought from home, and tons of hardcover and paperback books strewn across the floor. A parade of the smallest china animals I'd ever seen was lined up on her bed, and I admired the fact that none were broken or chipped. Give me one minute with those critters and, smash, I'd probably end up sitting on them by mistake.

Phoebe's cheerful outlook on most everything irritated me. In fact, it irritated me a lot. Didn't she realize that she'd been abandoned by her parents and left under the care of a cooking maniac? Couldn't she see that Beach Bluff was dark as a dungeon and falling apart at the seams? I couldn't believe that my brother's freedom depended on this kid. What if I couldn't get her to agree to my brilliant new idea and I was wasting my time, sitting around with a bunch of old books and little fragile creatures?

One afternoon, I spied a black-and-white-splattered composition notebook in Phoebe's bedroom, just like the ones we used in school, crammed in on one shelf, but when I reached for it, Phoebe grabbed it right out of my hands.

"That's private," she said, lowering her eyes. "No fair looking." Although she stuck the notebook under her pillow real fast, I glimpsed the name written in large letters on the front cover, PHOEBE D. SINCLAIR, over the words KEEP OUT, with what looked like five or six huge exclamation marks. You could be sure that the *keep out* instructions made me want to take an immediate peek since there's nothing more tempting than being told to keep out. I mean, come on.

I guess I wouldn't want anyone looking over my school composition books either since I wasn't much of a speller and my homework was marked everywhere with the dreaded red pen. Writing "mechanics" weren't my thing. Funny, because I was pretty darn good with anything mechanical outside of school; I was a beast at fixing bikes, fishing rods, even my mother's washer and dryer.

I watched Phoebe put her composition book under her pillow and smiled as she showed me all her special trinkets. Three small tin boxes of her "treasures" had been packed in her suitcases from home. The boxes were red and silver, with the word *Altoids* spelled out on top. It was hard to believe that anything so tiny could actually fit something inside, but when Phoebe opened those barely-there boxes to show me, I was surprised. The first was filled with miniature marbles, the second with colorful bite-sized beads, and the third with four baby teeth.

"Not mine," Phoebe assured me, as if I cared. "They're my great-grandmother's. She lived here once."

Suddenly, I did care.

"Wait," I said, my head spinning. "Wait, I thought you were only renting Beach Bluff."

"We are, silly."

"Then how come your great-grandmother lived here?"

"Didn't I tell you? Because my great-grandfather grew up on Rock Haven and so he and my great-grandmother bought Beach Bluff when they got married. But they sold it a long time ago after their little baby daughter died. And Mother remembered staying here when she was a child ages ago and decided that it would be nice to rent it for this summer."

I didn't know what to say. Great-grandmothers, dead

children, and old baby teeth? Was it my imagination, or did the silver-and-red tin box lying on my palm begin to tremble or was it my own hand?

"Here, give me that back, Beanie." Phoebe grabbed the box from me, something I considered to be pretty rude. "I wouldn't want my great-grandmother's baby teeth to get lost somewhere in the house. It would be real creepy to find an old tooth somewhere when you weren't even expecting it!"

I couldn't have agreed with her more.

It was the very next day after finding Phoebe's great-grandmother's teeth that my lunches at Beach Bluff came to an abrupt end. This had nothing to do with Phoebe, but with my growing suspicion that something was very, very wrong at the house.

I'd been doing my best to cement my friendship with Phoebe, so that she'd go along with what I wanted to do in order to make my much-needed bail cash.

That is, until we started hearing the voices.

Now, I'm not the kind of kid who believes in ghosts or haunted houses, but something was definitely not right at Beach Bluff. I didn't know if this had to do with Phoebe's great-grandparents and their dead little girl or with the strange nanny and his Down Under ways.

The first time we heard the voices, Phoebe and I were minding our own business, riffling through one of the ten trunks

Phoebe's parents had shipped to Rock Haven. We'd dragged a real heavy one all the way from the hall closet into Phoebe's bedroom, and we were both pretty tired when we were done. It was the end of an entire week of doing whatever Phoebe wanted, and I lay back on her bed, trying to keep my patience.

Phoebe was determined to find some kind of bathing suit to squeeze Honey into, an impossible job, but you couldn't really get the kid to change her mind once she'd glommed on to something. I could see that she was getting frustrated as she sifted through a bunch of men's clothes, one hand in her mouth, and began to gnaw away at her pitiful fingernails. She was wearing orange-and-yellow tie-dyed overalls with a red T-shirt underneath and her curly hair twisted into three unruly braids. Why three? I didn't even bother to ask.

But I took the opportunity to bring up her getting a puppy again, reminding Phoebe how much fun it would be to dress up a pretty little dog instead of the hulking Honey. She just nodded slowly, then, to my irritation, turned right back to the subject of bathing suits.

"Where are the bikinis?" she whined. "Where are Mother's bathing suits? I know she packed a bunch, and Honey really, really needs them."

I wasn't so sure about that.

And that's just when we heard it. Right then and there. First a faint, barely audible squeal, and then a tiny, high-pitched cry, sounding like a small child was locked up somewhere and couldn't find her way out. Such a barely-there sound, but loud enough so that we both looked at each other at the same time in alarm, our eyes open wide.

"Shhh," I whispered as Phoebe started to speak. "Shhh, let's see if we can hear it again."

Then nothing.

"Maybe it was one of the pipes," I said, not entirely convinced. "Sometimes old houses like this have creaky kinds of plumbing."

We sat there for another few minutes just listening. Absolute quiet. I was beginning to feel silly, the two of us frozen in silence. Soon, we went back to bathing suit trunk shopping and forgot about the noise.

Later that same afternoon, we found a pair of Phoebe's father's navy swimming trunks, although we couldn't seem to pull them over Honey's rump. But I knew better than to say anything about that tight squeeze.

"Don't ever call her fat," Phoebe told me once, sharply. "She's just big boned."

The very next day, I was using the upstairs bathroom at Beach Bluff, the one wallpapered with dark green-and-purple roses and that always smelled funny, like mothballs mixed with cough syrup. I liked using that particular bathroom because it was at the top of a back stairway that led straight to the kitchen, so I didn't have to walk down any dark, creepy hallway. Phoebe told me that Beach Bluff actually had six full bathrooms, something I found incredible but still didn't doubt. The rose wallpaper one was right next to Phoebe's bedroom, where we usually hung out, and it made me feel at ease to see her clothes haphazardly strewn about on the black-and-white diamond-shaped tile floor. Most of the other rooms in Beach Bluff, bathrooms or not, gave me the creeps.

During this particular bathroom visit, however, I discovered that Beach Bluff really might actually be haunted and my initial impressions of the house were right-on. Minding my own business, I turned on the water to wash my hands, reaching for the pink soap that was shaped like a fish. The old porcelain faucet squeaked as the water ran and then kept squeaking after I turned it off. I swallowed hard but didn't move an inch. Actually the sound was more like the littlest voice, a wail rather than a squeak, and then a rustling and the wailing all over again. The sound was so soft, hardly there at all, that I thought it might be my imagination playing tricks on me, but when I put my ear to the wall, I jumped back to the other side of the room. I had definitely heard a tiny voice, someone or something crying out.

I got out of there as fast as I could, directly downstairs into the kitchen, where Edwin was serving Phoebe a second helping of seared tuna with orange-ginger sauce.

"What's wrong?" Phoebe immediately stopped eating. "Are you feeling sick again?"

I didn't say anything for a minute but tumbled into a chair. All my limbs felt rubbery, boneless. A line of hives popped, one by one, across my chest.

Once I thought Edwin had left the kitchen, I turned to her and whispered, "I heard them again. The voices."

"What? What voices?"

"The ones we heard upstairs in the bedroom the other day. THE VOICES."

"Are you sure? Are you really, really sure?" Phoebe's eyes widened and her mouth dropped open. I could see a few pieces of chewed tuna sloshing around inside.

"You know, children, it's rude to whisper. Unless you're at a place of worship or a funeral, that is." And so there he was again, the ever-present nanny, appearing out of thin air, like a red-haired ghost, a large ladle in one hand and an eggplant in the other. How in the world did he manage to do it—show up without making a sound? Not normal, if you ask me.

A shiver raced up my spine.

"Edwin"—Phoebe looked aggravated—"it's not polite to eavesdrop and we weren't whispering, anyway? Just talking quietly. This is private stuff between Beanie and me."

Edwin just gave her a quick shrug and exited the room as soundlessly as he arrived.

CHAPTER TWELVE

I decided right then and there that, no matter what, I wouldn't ever set foot inside Beach Bluff again. After all, it was the second incident of voices and I didn't see the point of pretending anymore that the old house didn't have dark spirits flitting about. Everything pointed to that. And it really wasn't a matter of believing that the voices were real or not; I knew what I heard with my own ears and knew what I felt every single time I entered the big, old, creaky house.

It was time to put my plan for getting my hands on some cash into action anyway, so it really didn't make any difference if I spent more time inside or not. As long as Phoebe agreed to Honey's sale, all would be fine and I'd never again have to walk through Beach Bluff's front door. Although I had to admit that I would kind of miss the lunches.

Phoebe and I had been hanging out together most of the time by then, and I pretty much had her wrapped around my finger, being older and knowing all about Rock Haven stuff. I'd already taught her how to find sea glass on the short, rocky Refuge Beach down the hill from Beach Bluff; the best places to go swimming once the water warmed up a bit; where to dig for quahogs; how to spot dolphins and from which ledge. For some reason, though, I didn't want to take her fishing—that was something special for just for my brother and me. But I could tell that Phoebe was beginning to look up to me, fishing or not, since she pretty much followed me around without question. So now that the time had finally come to put my plan into motion, I had a feeling that there was a good chance she'd play ball.

I'd realized, though, that once I'd gotten Phoebe to agree to selling Honey, I still might have some problems to iron out. For one, how would I actually put up the big dog for sale? Since I knew almost everyone on my island, or they knew my mother or brother, it would be pretty hard to make the sale without raising questions. And just imagining what would happen then made me shiver. My mother would punish me for the rest of my life, Phoebe's parents would be furious, and there'd be no end to the trouble. No doubt about it, I'd have to figure out some way to sell Honey without anyone finding out. Not easy, I can tell you that!

My inspiration for how to solve that problem came to me the very next day. After a long time on the porch discussing whether the voices we'd heard in the wall were real or not, Phoebe wanted to hunt for sea glass in the weedy grass around a nearby abandoned construction site, even though I'd told her again and again that the stuff could only be found on beaches. But Phoebe had insisted on a "treasure hunt" and so I went along just to keep her from driving me nuts. While we were sifting through the dirt and pebbles, I kept trying to bring up my idea of selling Honey for a new puppy, but she insisted on talking about her neighbor who'd been hurt in some kind of accident. She was determined to find him a pretty piece of glass as a gift, but I wasn't really listening, too annoyed at having to waste time looking for treasure when none was even there. And if, by some strange chance, I happened to find a good piece of glass, I sure wasn't going to give it to Phoebe's neighbor, I can tell you that. Some could bring in a good chunk of cash.

"You know," I said, watching her sift through the weeds, "most sea glass isn't worth anything, anyway. Just the orange or turquoise ones are real valuable."

"But I like all the colors," she'd insisted, proudly holding up a shard of Coke bottle.

"That's not sea glass, dummy, and you'd better be careful not to cut yourself." I didn't want to be rude but come on. Anyone could see the difference. "Real sea glass is colored and all smooth and stuff from being beaten up by the ocean for a long time. And I told you that we'll have to go down to the beach if you really want to find some."

"Well, why are orange and turquoise the most valuable?" Phoebe was clearly ignoring the important tidbit of information I'd just shared by slipping the piece of Coke bottle into her pocket.

"I dunno. They just are."

"Let's look it up on the computer." She smiled at me and brightened. "I don't have any books on sea glass, but Edwin has a computer we can use. We'll have to ask his permission."

While I had no interest in looking up anything to do with sea glass on Edwin's computer, an idea suddenly popped into my head about how to make the sale. And it had everything to do with the strange nanny and the laptop I'd seen him use from time to time. We could go online to advertise Honey's sale and get the money for bail without anyone finding out. Of course, we'd have to use the computer without the nanny's permission, considering my idea to sell the big dog wasn't exactly something he'd approve of, but a computer was the perfect way to find a buyer.

Using Edwin's computer would be the beginning of my brilliant idea to rescue Willis from jail.

Sometimes, I surprised myself with my own smarts.

But before I could even bring up the subject of selling Honey to get Phoebe a new puppy, she decided to challenge me to a race back up the bluff, something I couldn't resist. "Hurry, Beanie," she called to me. "We gotta get back to help Edwin with all that baking."

Baking? I had a plan to present and no idea why Phoebe suddenly had baking, of all things, in mind. But when she ran past me at the speed of light, I couldn't resist taking off after her. Of course, I probably should have let the kid win, but it was too tempting to leave her in the dust.

When Phoebe eventually caught up to me in front of Beach

Bluff, she kept on running all the way right into the house. "Come on," Phoebe called without looking back, "let's get to baking and then do some secret exploring inside the walls, if you know what I mean." She leapt over the snoozing Honey and up the porch steps.

Of course I knew what she meant. I knew exactly what she meant, and I wasn't interested, still freaked out by what I had heard in the walls the day before. But it was important that I explain my new plan to Phoebe, although I had no intention of going inside the house. A few hives made their way across my left wrist, and I felt a wave of vertigo coming on. *Just nerves*, I told myself. *Just nerves.*

So, instead of following Phoebe into Beach Bluff, I decided to take a few minutes for myself to think about the best way to finally present my entire brilliant plan. I knew the time had come, and I couldn't delay anymore. But it wasn't going to be easy and I wasn't sure what Phoebe's response would be.

When I'd calmed myself down and felt ready, I walked around the house, hoping to find Phoebe on the back porch, but no such luck. She didn't answer when I called out her name from outside either, so taking a deep breath, I knocked on the kitchen door. Nothing. I knocked again.

"Come on in! I'm busy baking."

I could tell by her tone that she was irritated. And, despite my sacred oath to never again set a foot inside the old place, I screwed up my courage and opened the door slowly, peering around carefully. I didn't know which was worse on my nerves:

the thought of revealing my plan to Phoebe or going back inside the very place where I'd heard voices in the walls. But sunlight swept into the kitchen, as if lighting a path, so I walked slowly ahead to find Edwin and Phoebe arguing at the sink. About one hundred sugar cookies, of all things.

They were facing each other, both rattling some bowls and pans. The counters and kitchen table were covered with open cookbooks, eggshells, flour, and a spreading mound of confectioners' sugar. "Hurry, Beanie," Phoebe said once she saw me, turning to the big copper bowl on the table. She whipped out a long wooden spoon sticking out of her apron pocket and began stirring ferociously. "Edwin already got started, even though he promised he was going to wait until I got back. You can help if you want."

"What's up?" I noticed Edwin pushing a cookie sheet into the oven and then giving Phoebe a pleading look. "Looks like a pretty big mess." I could immediately tell that my talking to Phoebe about Honey right then wasn't going to happen.

"That's pan number two," Edwin told her, wiping his brow with his shirtsleeve. "How many are you planning to make?"

"Ten," Phoebe answered without skipping a beat. "Ten pans times ten cookies for each sheet is . . . one hundred!"

"What are you doing?" The kitchen was filling up with the smell of sugar and butter, making my mouth water. "Why do you need one hundred cookies?"

Now Phoebe was spooning out the dough onto the cookie sheet, the front of her pink blouse white with flour. "Oh," she said happily, as if about to share good news. "I told you about Mr. Spencer, our neighbor, having an accident. Edwin found out that he actually sprained his ankle really badly, so I decided to bake him some cookies. I guess he has a nurse now but mostly lives alone in that big house and probably hasn't had any homemade cookies for a real long time." She was breathless after her long speech, her cheeks pink and her hair wild in the humid kitchen air. I thought it kinda strange that she was smiling while telling me about her neighbor's accident. But Phoebe was the kind of person who was happy when helping someone. I hadn't known her long, but I somehow figured that was the case.

"But we *will not* be making one hundred cookies," Edwin said curtly. "Four pans of ten will be more than enough."

"But what about his nurse?" Phoebe wiped off her face with a paper towel as if competing in the annual Rock Haven marathon. "She might get hungry too."

"Four trays, forty cookies. That's all and that's final." Edwin's voice was low, and it was clear there was no room for argument.

I suddenly remembered the man in the pinstripe suit who shook my hand at Reel Paradise when I was looking for work. "You mean the old guy who lives in Reel Paradise?"

"Yes," Phoebe said quickly. "Do you know him? Edwin and I were walking by last night and saw him trip right on his very own porch steps. We got him back onto the porch, and Edwin called the doctor who's renting Sea-esta down the street to help out. Hey, Beanie, do you know that in some countries, once you save someone's life, you're responsible for them forever, do you know that, Beanie, do you?"

Actually, I did know that. Willis had told me all about it one day last summer when we were fishing together off the jetty at Halibut Beach. We usually didn't go all the way over to that side of the island, but that day, Willis got a ride and brought me along.

"Hold your pole steady, sis," he had told me, "and don't let the line pop off the reel again like you did last time. And let's throw back everything we catch today, no matter what size. Just for today."

"Why?" I'd asked, annoyed. If I actually caught a big one, there was no way I wanted to throw it back.

"Because," Willis had answered, balancing carefully on a jetty rock, his sneakers already soaked at the toes, "if we save the fish, then we'll have to watch over them forever, make sure that they'll always be there in our island water. You know, that's the way it is in some cultures. I once read that there are folks who believe that if you rescue someone or something, you're responsible for keeping them safe forever, no matter what."

I'd mulled it over back then, the sun rolling over my face and the wind making it more and more difficult not to slip on the wet jumble of rocks. I'd thought that it was a lot to ask, watching over the fish forever and ever, and worried whether I was up to the task. Did this mean I'd always have to throw back every single one I caught? That just didn't seem reasonable.

And now, Phoebe was telling me the same thing about the man next door. I was sure that I didn't want to be responsible for him either.

"Well," I finally told her, "I didn't do the saving, so I guess it's up to you and Edwin to keep the old guy safe. But I could help you bake if you let me have a spoonful of that dough to taste." It was clear that this wasn't going to be the morning I'd get to share my plan with Phoebe, and I was both frustrated and relieved. Frustrated because everything had to be set in motion as soon as possible and relieved because I dreaded talking to her about such a delicate subject.

So Edwin, Phoebe, and I spent the morning icing forty just-baked sugar cookies for Mr. Spencer and his nurse. Well, actually thirty-four, if you didn't count the ones the three of us ate.

Finally, it was time to face Phoebe with my plan. "Hey," I said to her that afternoon, trying to sound as casual as possible, my stomach knotted and my voice kinda shaky. "I have a good idea about how you could get a pretty little puppy. You still want a puppy, don't you?" No more putting it off. Willis had been in jail two weeks. It was time to finally put my plan into action.

Phoebe stopped in her tracks. We'd been walking down the road to the Coastal Convenience Mart, where I'd promised to buy her an ice cream sandwich and pick up some almond milk for Edwin, who had given me two five-dollar bills.

"Don't forget to bring back the change," he'd growled, as if I was planning to hightail it somewhere off island with his ten dollars. Anyway, I highly doubted that Coastal carried soy or almond milk.

"What are you talking about, Beanie? Do you mean that you know of a puppy I could get? How?" Phoebe asked breathlessly. "A little puppy? Really? How? Did Edwin say it was okay? Did he write my parents?"

"Not exactly." I knew I had to play my cards carefully. The kid might have only been nine, but she still was pretty smart and might need a bunch of convincing. It was a real hot day, beads of sweat forming on my forehead and upper lip; well, maybe I wasn't exactly sweating from the afternoon sun. I turned my head, pretending to look over the street toward the ocean.

"Then what, exactly?"

"Well, you'd have to keep a secret. Can you keep a secret so we can buy you a pretty dog?" My head was still turned away, so she couldn't see the flush creeping up from my neck to my face. I knew that I sounded like an idiot, like I was talking to some tiny baby or toddler, instead of a nine-year-old girl. Finally, I turned back to her.

Phoebe looked confused for a minute and then peeved. "Not a dog, Beanie. A puppy. I want a little puppy."

"Okay, okay, same deal." It was clear that Phoebe was no pushover, that was for sure. "Look," I continued, looking straight at her, "I can get you any puppy you want, but there's something we have to do first." We were still standing in the street, so I pulled her over to the curb to give her all the gory details.

"What? What would I have to do?"

Was it my imagination or did Phoebe look a tad suspicious? Her freckled face was screwed up in a mixture of impatience and excitement, and her eyes were blinking furiously.

"Think about this for a minute. Do you get to walk Honey or carry her around like the girls in the movies?"

"You know I can't. Honey's too big. Stop being silly, Beanie."

I took a deep breath. Now wasn't the time to lose my temper. Best to go straight to the point.

"What if we found Honey another home, sold her to a nice, new family, since she's worth so much money, and used some of the cash to buy you the exact puppy you want? What do you think about that?"

"Sell Honey?"

I nodded. Silence for a moment, then: "I'm not so sure about that. I like Honey."

"Wouldn't you rather have a puppy?"

"But what would Edwin say?"

I was prepared for this question, having gone over Phoebe's possible responses in my head again and again the night before.

"Edwin might even be happy since he hates feeding and walking Honey and always complains about her drooling all over the place and about her stinky farts."

"But what will my parents say?"

I was prepared for this one too.

"Your parents won't be back for a while, and by the time they return, you'll have trained your new puppy to do so many great tricks that they'll be fine. In fact, they'll be happy. Your puppy won't smell gross the way Honey does and won't eat as much food, so it'll be cheaper to take care of and its poop will be smaller. What do you think? Are you in or are you out?"

Phoebe looked uncertain for a minute, twirling one foot in a mound of sandy dirt. She was wearing pointed silver cowboy boots that looked ridiculous with her purple shorts and pink blouse.

"Phoebe?"

"I'm in!" she yelled, all of a sudden hugging me so hard that I found it hard to breathe. "Let's get a real pretty white puppy for me to walk and carry around all day!"

And so the deed was done. It seemed that Phoebe really was on board. All systems were go.

CHAPTER THIRTEEN

But as it turned out, all systems weren't go at all, and there was a giant hitch in getting my plan underway.

And it was Phoebe, the one person I needed on my side, who turned out to be that very hitch.

Even though she'd agreed to my plan of selling Honey for her puppy just the day before, she seemed to be more interested in the problems of her neighbor. She'd seen a wheelchair being delivered to Reel Paradise early that morning and gotten it into her head that Mr. Spencer needed a way to wheel himself up and down the porch stairs. Apparently, she figured that Edwin was the perfect person to help her.

"Why me?" Edwin complained early that morning as he studied something in a white pot on the stove. Whatever he was making smelled good, filling up Beach Bluff's kitchen with a comforting scent. "I'm not a carpenter and have my own work to do. I'm pretty sure that the old man has someone else to help him with that kind of thing."

"Who?" Phoebe could be pretty pushy when she wanted to and, for a brief second, I almost felt sorry for Edwin. I'd learned that once Phoebe got something in her head, there was no turning back. "Who's going to help him if we don't?"

"I don't know, Phoebe," Edwin whined, dramatically rubbing his forehead. "Mr. Spencer must have someone, or at least know someone who could make a ramp."

"But what if he doesn't? I know he has a nurse, but nurses don't know how to build stuff. How is he ever going to get out of the house? What if there's a fire and there's no way to escape? You know," she said solemnly, grabbing one of Edwin's hands, "you're responsible for him too. You were with me when we saw Mr. Spencer fall, and it was you who called for help."

"I'm sure he has someone to help with his wheelchair, Phoebe. Someone he hired to give him a hand." A trickle of white foam slid out of the pot that Edwin was stirring, and he sighed heavily.

"But that's the point. How can he get out of the house in his wheelchair? How can he get down the front steps? A wheelchair is too heavy to carry, especially if someone is sitting in it, so even if someone else is around, he'd be stuck inside."

The nonstop argument began to get on my nerves after a while, and it didn't take long for me to realize that Phoebe was never going to give up. Although I didn't really care how much she tortured Edwin, by lunchtime, I was pretty sick of the whole subject. I was ready to split a gut, desperately needing to talk to Phoebe about getting started on my plan, but it looked like she wouldn't listen to anything before helping the old man.

"I'll do it, Phoebe," I finally said, watching Edwin ladle out our lunch of cold cucumber soup and tiny boiled potatoes on the side. I'd never had cold soup before, and the light green mixture didn't look particularly tasty. "Making a ramp is pretty easy, and I can get my hands on a bunch of tools. But you have to promise me that this will be the end of helping Mr. Spencer. Remember, we've talked about a bunch of other important things to do." I was tempted to wink but decided otherwise since Edwin was in the room.

It was pretty aggravating that I'd have to take time out of putting my plan into action, but I knew that if I wanted Phoebe on my side, I'd just have to keep her happy.

Nobody said anything.

"I'll do it," I said again, in a louder voice. "Did either of you hear me? I said I'll build the darn ramp."

Edwin and Phoebe both looked up at me with the same expression on their faces, and it wasn't exactly confidence.

It only took us a few hours to make Mr. Spencer's ramp, but those hours were filled with pretty hard work. First of all, I had to figure out where to get the needed wood, and second of all, I didn't have my brother around to help. Any time I'd built anything in the past—a rack for Willis's bike, a cage for the mouse I found when I was nine, or the oblong skunk traps we'd shoved under our house—Willis had been there to show me what to do and help out. This time, I'd have to handle things on my own. Although I'd told Phoebe that I was a whiz at carpentry, making a ramp really wasn't as easy as I'd said and it took me a while to even figure out how to get started.

Luckily, I remembered seeing some scrap pieces of plywood left in the trash outside the construction site at the bluff's end when we were searching for sea glass. Everyone in town had been talking about this strange blotch of land since last summer; the property was owned by some famous football player from somewhere down south, and each time I walked by the barbed wire and chain-link fences surrounding the construction, I wondered who that might be. I also wondered why in the world it was taking so long to build the house—it was a real eyesore; a gigantic hole of mud and concrete blocks; a huge, swampy mess; and kind of pitiful too. Edwin had recently told me he'd learned that the town had temporarily stopped construction because the framing wasn't to code, and when I asked him what that meant, he shrugged and said something about the house plans being too big for the lot and that inspectors found that the foundation wasn't solid but cracked at the core.

Towanda, the new clerk at Coastal, told me that the football player was known to "play the horses," although I didn't really know what that meant. "Poor animals," she'd said, snapping her gum and taking my fifty cents for the cherry Tootsie Pop in my hand. "I just hate to think of those horses running their hearts out. It's unnatural. But guess there's a lot of money to be made and money makes the word go round."

I wasn't so sure about that. I didn't have more than ten dollars to my name and my world kept going round and round, even though I wanted it to stop.

Phoebe agreed to help me drag the plywood for the ramp

from the construction site all the way back to Reel Paradise, but first I had to warn her not to stick her face too close to the barbed wire that covered the chain-link fence in front of the muddy pit. Funny how someone so smart in so many ways could be so clueless. One touch to that barbed wire might cut right though her cheek, not to speak of the barbs getting caught on the sleeves of her dress. But when Phoebe looked at that big, empty hole where the new house was supposed to be, she just couldn't resist pressing up close. I could almost see her imagination billowing out from her mind like smoke.

"It's going to be wonderful!" She finally grinned, turning to me. "That house is going to be big, a perfect place for some family, Beanie, don't you think? I bet they'll have tons of kids with all kinds of pets living there too."

It made me sad to hear Phoebe say that. Really nothing but a gloomy mess of cement and mud on the other side, nothing but an empty ditch. I saw empty where she saw full. I saw an abandoned shell where she saw a home. Maybe Phoebe didn't know what an actual home looked like, her parents gone so often, no brothers or sisters, only nannies to take care of her. Maybe her imagination was wishful thinking. Somehow, I had the sudden urge to tell my friend about Willis's arrest right then and there and about how lonely I'd been without him. Thank goddess that the urge just lasted a second.

The walk back with the plywood wasn't really that far, but still tiring, although Phoebe was surprisingly strong, wearing a determined look on her face as we hobbled back up the bluff.

But I also could tell that she needed to rest when we finally finished carrying the wood, so I told her to sit down while I raced home to get Willis's old tool belt, hunched over and forgotten in one of our kitchen cabinets.

Cutting the plywood wasn't a problem and I used the mid-sized hand saw, since its worn green handle felt secure and its teeth still seemed pretty sharp. I'd left some of the other saws back at my house because they were either too rusty or too big for my hands. Willis had once built a small ramp for his skateboard and I remember him saying something about making certain that the slope was safe and the wood secure. It looked like I'd have to make sure that every inch upward of Mr. Spencer's ramp equaled at least one foot of rise, the way my brother had taught me, so Phoebe helped hold the plywood as I used my thumb to measure each inch. For some reason, the tool belt was missing Willis's measuring tape, but he'd always said that a thumb could be used as a pretty good measurement in its place. One inch per adult thumb so I just doubled mine.

Next, I sawed off a long strip of plywood and then nailed it back on to the end of the ramp with Willis's nail gun, making poor Phoebe jump with every pop. I tried with all my might to get the sawed-off strip to lie nailed-down flat on Reel Paradise's top step, but it wasn't exactly easy to get the narrow piece to stay put, and it ended up drifting over at an unfortunate slant. But who said the thing had to be perfect, anyway?

Once I was finally finished, I thought the ramp looked pretty sharp, sanded nicely where it had splintered, even though it hugged the porch steps crookedly. So what if it lay there at an uneven angle and if the bottom edge didn't completely reach the ground? But I was still worried about the flimsy wood and how it swayed when we tested it by jiggling it to and fro. What if the ramp slipped off the stairs when Mr. Spencer was heading out or shifted in place in the rain? Phoebe was right; the old man definitely needed a safe way to escape if there was a fire and no one was around. Quickly, I figured out how to get the ramp edges secured with some plain old sheet metal screws and flattened shanks. Willis had a ton of them stored in the middle tool-belt pocket.

Next, another problem. Since the plywood was pretty thin, I realized that it might not hold all that much weight. Poor Mr. Spencer and his wheelchair might just go flying up and out into the great beyond if I couldn't find a way to brace it with something real strong. Remembering some old pilings on the small strip of sand near Refuge Beach, I convinced Phoebe to help me lug one up back the hill. The short section I chose wasn't all that big but definitely heavier than I'd thought, and we had to stop every few minutes to catch our breath. Once we made it all the way back to Reel Paradise, we both flopped on the ground by our newly constructed ramp and sighed at the same time.

"How are we going to get that heavy thing underneath?" Phoebe asked me, still breathless.

I had to admit that I was pretty impressed with the kid. Not only had she helped me haul the piling and plywood, but she had also done some sanding on her own, working so hard that a cloud of filmy sawdust blew up into her face, making her sneeze. Now she was already eager to do even more. As I watched her adjust the torn neckline of her pink gauze dress, she looked up with an enormous smile. Her face was glistening with sweat, both cheeks smudged with dirt, and her chin had grown a yellow beard where she'd accidentally dipped it in wood shavings. I laughed.

"What's so funny?" She leapt up and shook herself off like a wet dog, both arms out at her sides. "Hurry up, Beanie. We've got more work to do."

The piling was pocked with holes from ocean water, making it look like an enormous piece of driftwood. But I knew, just by poking at it with the corner of a large seashell, that once the chunk of wood was dug into the ground, it would make the ramp much stronger. So, with Phoebe's help, I dragged and then shoved the waterlogged wood under the ramp. Next, I used a small shovel to dig out a long, rectangular pit and pushed in the bottom for support. When it was done, I looked up to grin at Phoebe and saw a woman staring down at us from Reel Paradise's front door. She wasn't smiling.

"May I help you? You do realize, don't you, children, that this is private property?" The woman had black hair slicked over to one side and was dressed in a crisp white shirt and white pants. Even her shoes were white.

"Mr. Spencer's nurse!" Phoebe whispered to me.

"We're just building something for the wheelchair," I said quickly, rubbing some dirt off my hands. "For Mr. Spencer, I mean. So he can go up and down."

The nurse looked at the ramp carefully and then at the two of us. For a minute, she seemed bewildered, but then inched out a bitter smile, exposing a row of large, perfectly white teeth. I immediately thought of the horse I used to ride at Yara Silva's aunt's farm mid-island. The same teeth, although they'd been yellow, not white. "You did this all by yourself, just the two of you?"

Phoebe and I nodded quickly. A bead of sweat ran down from my forehead into one eye, making it sting.

"And Mr. Spencer gave you his permission?"

"Well," I said, "not exactly . . ."

"Then I suggest you both remove yourself from the property immediately. Not only are you making a mess, but you're making so much noise that the gentleman isn't able to nap. And in any case, we've ordered a metal ramp from New England Medical Supplies off island, so that is that. And now," she continued under her breath, "I'll have to get them to get rid of this ugly thing."

I thought that the nurse was pretty darn rude, considering, and I picked up my tools slowly, sliding them back into the tool-belt pockets as calm as could be, but felt my temper rising up burning hot. After all that work, and not even a thank-you? And after taking important time away from getting Willis out of jail? Who did that woman think she was? "Hold on," my brother used to tell me when I got fighting mad. "Take a sec and hold on, sis. No point in losing your cool." I breathed deeply. I knew it wouldn't do me any good to be rude, since the nurse was right about our being on private property and my family certainly didn't need any more trouble with the law. But inside I was fuming and could also see that Phoebe was upset. Her bottom lip quivered, and both hands were clenched. We looked at each other for a minute, and then slowly started back next door to Beach Bluff. I could feel the nurse watching us as we walked away and then felt Phoebe take my hand.

"I sure wouldn't want that lady to take care of me," she murmured under her breath.

Phoebe's hand in mine felt tiny, and for some reason I thought of the baby bluebirds I'd spotted in the nest in the eaves under Reel Paradise's front porch. I flashed on Mr. Spencer's nurse again and wondered how she could even help sick people if she was so darn mean. I figured that I could do a better job of nursing than her, since I'd be nice to my patients and to any children who might be around, and then I wondered what it really would be like to take care of the sick like she did, spooning out medicine and checking for fevers. Of course, I'd be very kind and bring my patients all kinds of treats and gifts, maybe even a baby bluebird that had been left behind by its mother. It wasn't right to take the babies away from the parents, and I'd never even touch one unless it had been abandoned. But those little birds left behind definitely needed a gentle touch, someone to feed and care for them.

I looked over at Phoebe as we opened Beach Bluff's gate, and she greeted Honey, who was napping in the front yard where she always was since Edwin never allowed her inside the

house, except at night where she was confined to the front hallway. Phoebe's parents had made this rule, I guess to make sure
that Honey was always guarding the property and that she
wouldn't ever make a mess inside the house. Damaging furni-
ture or something. Not difficult to imagine that happening
considering her gigantic size and the tons and tons of drool!

Phoebe's hand slipped from mine and she stumbled, then
turned back to me, her expression solemn.

"Thanks for helping me make the ramp, Beanie," she said.
"It stinks that the nurse was so awful and Mr. Spencer won't
get to use it, but at least we got the job done. I just couldn't
stand the thought of anyone trapped inside that big house with
no way out. Even if they end up using another ramp, well, at
least we tried and Mr. Spencer will be safe."

We had gotten the job done, that was true. And together
we'd made something really nice for someone who needed it,
without anybody's help, not even my brother's. It had been
Phoebe's idea to build a ramp for Mr. Spencer and mine to use
the plywood and the piling. I'd known how to build something
sturdy using Willis's tools, but together, Phoebe and I had given
the old man a way to stay safe.

Later, as I was bringing a small bowl of cranberry juice out to
Honey as Phoebe had instructed, I saw a white envelope that
had been slipped under the door. When I picked it up, I was
surprised at how heavy it felt and even more surprised to see

what was written on the front. The word *Children* in dark blue ink with a tiny, stray splotch at one corner.

When I called Phoebe over to look at it, she took the envelope in both hands and stood very still. "I think it must be from Mr. Spencer," she said quietly. "I hope he's not mad that we made him a ramp he didn't need." Then she slit open the envelope with her index finger, and a photograph floated to the floor. It was black and white, and yellowed at the corners, smaller than any photo I'd ever seen before, maybe only an inch or so wide. When we looked at it together, I saw a picture of a boy with a small dog. The boy was wearing a cap, one of those old-fashioned ones that kind of puffed up in the center with a pointed brim, and the dog was coal black, his muzzle in the boy's hand.

Phoebe handed me the photograph and then the paper that had also been folded inside. It was thick and a creamy tan color, more like cardboard than paper. In the same shaky writing:

> Children,
> Thank you for your help.
> Please take good care of your
> impressive dog.
> > Cordially,
> > Mr. Eugene R. Spencer, Esquire

Two twenty-dollar bills were taped underneath.

"Wow, twenty dollars each! That's a whole bunch of cash!" I couldn't believe my eyes and immediately thought about where to stash it for Willis's bail. "Hey, do you know what the word *esquire* means?" I asked Phoebe, figuring it would be the kind of thing she'd know, but she only shrugged.

"Dunno," she replied softly, looking at the small photograph again. "Maybe it's a royal title like duke or prince."

"And why do you think he sent us the photograph?"

She shrugged again and looked up with a watery smile. "I guess that Mr. Spencer wanted us to know, a long time ago, he had an animal to love all his own."

CHAPTER FOURTEEN

No more time for dilly-dallying with cookies and ramps, and no more time to waste before finally getting my plan underway. I had put in my time working to stay on Phoebe's good side with sea glass hunts, cookies, and ramps. Now was finally the time for action.

So, on the afternoon after building Mr. Spencer's ramp, once we had cleaned up and had our lunch, I decided to finally explain the first few steps of my plan to Phoebe. We sat outside on the front porch so that Edwin wouldn't overhear us, and I carefully went over exactly what we'd have to do for Phoebe to get her very own puppy. The first step would be getting hold of Edwin's computer to advertise Honey's sale.

Phoebe looked upset at first, then confused, and then started gnawing on her left hand's fingernails, so I decided I'd better break down everything for her step by step.

Step one: Borrow Edwin's computer while he naps.

Step two: Get online pronto.

Step three: Advertise Honey on Craigslist.

Step four: Sell Honey for three thousand dollars.

Step five: Get Phoebe her puppy.

Phoebe most certainly didn't have to know about step four

and one half: Use one thousand dollars of the money to get Willis out of jail. There are some things better kept to yourself.

While I absolutely understood what we were doing was pretty sleazy, I comforted myself by figuring that it was all for the greater good. And I didn't have any intention of keeping any cash from Honey's sale for myself; Phoebe could use the remaining two thousand to buy the little puppy she'd wanted and anything else, for that matter.

But, wouldn't you know, even though I'd worked so hard to get her to trust me, Phoebe immediately started to object, and I could see that I might have my hands full.

"But what if she doesn't want to go?" She lifted her right hand and stared at it, as if the bony thing might belong to someone else. Then, after a few seconds, started her usual fingernail attack.

"Who?"

"Honey. What if she doesn't want to be sold to a stranger and go live with someone else? And you saw Mr. Spencer's note. We need to take good care of her. Think about it, Beanie; what if Honey wants to stay home at Beach Bluff?"

I had to admit that Phoebe had me there. I hadn't considered Honey's feelings—wait, she was just a dog and a simpleminded one at that. Chances were she didn't have any real feelings or thoughts, anyway. I had to think quickly to avoid a complete disaster. Luckily, I came up with something right away.

"Well, what if we sell Honey to a place that has a real big yard or meadow where she can run around and play?"

"She never runs or plays."

"But what if we sell her to someone who lets her roam free inside, you know, so she doesn't always have to be holed up in the front yard like she is here, somewhere she has a big, comfy dog bed? You know, like the one we saw in that catalog you like."

Phoebe was a huge catalog fan and a bunch were delivered to Beach Bluff's mailbox almost every week.

Just the other day, *Mostly Mutts* came our way and Phoebe started obsessing over a yellow-and-white-checked dog bed shaped like a heart.

"Maybe her new owners will let her hang out in their house and get her one of those fancy dog beds you're always talking about and all kinds of dog toys."

"And a matching blanket."

"Yes, and a matching blanket." I was nodding vigorously. "And maybe even dog booties for walking on rocks and when it snows." Phoebe had been talking my ear off about getting booties for Honey after seeing a little Pekingese strutting down the street with bright orange ones on its minuscule paws.

Phoebe looked at me suspiciously. "Well, okay, I guess," she muttered, "but you promise about the booties?"

It looked like my plan was finally underway.

I had to admit that step one of my idea to borrow the computer made me very nervous.

I knew that trying to sneak around behind Edwin's back

wasn't going to be easy and explained to Phoebe that we absolutely couldn't let him catch us or there'd be serious fallout. But this was a man who crept around the house silently in fleece slippers and had an odd way of turning up when you didn't even know he was there. He could easily overhear us talking and become suspicious. But I'd figured out how to avoid that happening.

After lunch, each and every day, Edwin would stretch out his big self on the wicker chaise on the back porch, a glass of lemonade in hand, and take a nap. Sometimes, we'd see him with a book or magazine open on his chest and then watch, giggling, when it slowly slid to the floor as he wheezed away. Once, Phoebe snuck up the back porch steps and put a blade of seagrass under Edwin's nose as he slept, and we both had trouble keeping our hysterics in check each time he sneezed.

This would be the time to use the laptop. He always had his slim silver laptop computer by his side on the small porch table. Phoebe said he used it to look up all kinds of recipes and take notes on every meal he made.

So, despite my nerves and a fat red hive on my neck, I felt pretty darn prepared when the next day came and my official life as a criminal began. I wasn't kidding myself; I knew right from wrong and knew that what I was doing was definitely wrong. Wrong to borrow Edwin's computer without his permission. Wrong to lie to Edwin. Wrong to lie to Phoebe. Very wrong to sell Honey. *So that's how criminals get started*, I thought to myself; it wasn't that they didn't know what they were doing was bad—it was just that they didn't care. Maybe that's what happened to Willis.

Edwin didn't snore while he slept but wheezed so loudly that anything in his general vicinity quivered. Even the pages of the open book (*New England Soups and Stews*) on his chest fluttered, giving the impression of being alive. In that moment, just as I crept up the back porch steps, Edwin reminded me of Honey. A bloated, potbellied creature, head lolling to one side, his belly heaving up and down with each breath. I had the sudden urge to put a pink bow on his head, just to finish off the picture.

But I had no time for such useless shenanigans. Phoebe was waiting for me in the kitchen, where I would meet her, and where we could work on the computer together and still have a clear view of Edwin in case he woke up suddenly. I tiptoed carefully across the porch floor, but to my horror, the old wood planks creaked under my bare feet, and for a minute, I thought I might faint from pure terror.

"Hang in, little buddy," Willis used to tell me when I was just a kid and scared of the dark. "Just take a few breaths and hang in."

So that's just what I did, took three deep breaths and pushed forward, right up to Edwin's side. Grabbing the laptop with both hands, I stumbled, almost falling onto the big belly right in front of me. Luckily, I regained my balance quickly, and Edwin didn't move one inch.

Phoebe was white as a sheet when I made it into the kitchen.

She was sitting at the table, drumming her fingers across the Formica.

"Got it?" she whispered.

"Got it."

Then, as quickly as possible, I opened the laptop, prepared to immediately pull up the Craigslist site. And then it hit me. Disaster. Something, stupidly, I hadn't considered. How could I have missed something so important?

"We don't have his password," I told Phoebe, panic flooding my entire body. "We can't get in without his password."

Phoebe just grinned and whispered, "*Risotto*. That's Edwin's favorite food and he told me that would be the password for the alarm system. I bet it's the same for his computer."

Alarm system? Beach Bluff had an alarm system and a guard dog? Chances were that neither were effective or even needed, for that matter. I typed in *Rissotto*. No luck. "How do you spell it?" I asked Phoebe, having no earthly idea what in the heck risotto even was. I quickly glanced out the window to see if Edwin was still asleep.

"R-I-S-O-T-T-O."

I tried it again. No luck. Time was running out.

Once more. This time with no capitals and snap, I was in.

But before I had the chance to log on to Craigslist, the laptop wallpaper popped up on the screen. It was a photograph of Edwin, but maybe a few years younger. And to my surprise, he was holding a little girl on his lap. She had red hair and looked about five or six. Both of them were smiling.

Come to think of it, I don't think I'd ever seen Edwin smile.

"He's getting up! He's getting up! Hurry, hurry, Beanie."

So I shut the computer and raced to the kitchen's back door. When I peered out into the porch, heart in mouth, I could see the green chaise move. *Hang in*, I told myself. *Just hang in.* And then, to my relief, I realized that Edwin had simply shifted in place and turned his head to one side. It must have taken me less than two minutes to replace the laptop on the round table and return to the kitchen, dripping with sweat.

Clearly, I wasn't cut out for a life of crime.

So back to square one, or to be more precise: step one.

CHAPTER FIFTEEN

My mother used to tell me that I tended to make my life as hard as possible—going to school without my lunch and then having to come home again to get it, beach-combing after washing up so I'd have to take another dreaded shower, doing my homework so late at night that I'd fall asleep at the square oak table and get a big fat F. I guess she may have been onto something since trying to use Edwin's computer was kinda pointless and definitely made my life more difficult than needed.

Because there was a computer sitting right there in the Rock Haven Public Library! One that was free for anyone to use. I didn't have to risk life and limb by borrowing Edwin's laptop and could have easily used the library computer in order to post Honey's ad on Craigslist. It aggravated me that I hadn't thought of this before, but I was also relieved at such a simple solution. So after updating Phoebe on this new development the very next day, I raced to town, making my way straight to the Rock Haven Public Library.

Generally, books weren't my thing and I found libraries boring as all get out. I immediately started to yawn as I walked through the narrow glass doors of the Rock Haven Public

Library. It was the absolute quiet that made me want to nod off right away. During the school year, we had a library period and were forced to check out books in order to give oral reports in class. I usually headed right for the sports section since the books there were shorter and sometimes had photographs of real baseball players or Olympic skiers.

There was a teenager in a college sweatshirt working intently on the library computer when I got there, so I had to wait around for a bit. Since I didn't know the guy (something rare in Rock Haven) I could afford to be kinda rude and started to sigh heavily and tap my feet loudly after a while. That was one good thing about summer on island; there were so many tourists crowding around everywhere that you could become invisible for once and be pretty sure that bad behavior wouldn't get back to your parents, or parent in my case. Off season, everyone knew everyone else's business and you'd better not screw up in public or a grounding would be coming your way pronto.

Once, I threw a Milky Way candy wrapper on the street when walking home from school, and by the time I got home, my mother was calling from the Stop & Shop to tell me that my Saturday plans would be squelched. Both Tommy Costa's and Yara Silva's mothers had seen me litter and immediately reported back to my mother at work. You really couldn't get away with too much on the island during off season.

Finally, Mr. College finished and, flashing him a dirty look, I hopped online. Quickly, I typed Honey's ad in the Craigslist Classifieds, using all the info Phoebe and Edwin had told me.

Mastiff Dog for Sale.

Rock Haven.

Champion.

Strong! Won in the ring. Descended from fighters.

$3,000 cash.

Call Dog Man Spike

at 555-879-8246.

Confidential. Call between 9:30 a.m. and

4:30 p.m. But don't leave messages.

I figured it was safe to give out our landline number, when my mother was at Stop & Shop. I'd plan on being home to pick up all the calls but would have to remember my pretend name. Spike seemed just right to me, since it sounded kinda tough, and if someone left a message after hours, despite my instructions, my mother might think it was a wrong number. I figured that just sitting at home all day, waiting for the phone to ring, was going to be really boring, but I didn't have a choice. It was worth it to get Willis out of jail.

When I told Phoebe the details of my outing at the library, her smile turned into a frown. "You promise that Honey will be okay and happy too? I don't want to sell her unless I'm sure of that."

I nodded.

"Because," she continued, looking carefully into my eyes, "all animals deserve good homes and to be treated really, really well."

I nodded again, but the outline of her face slowly started to blur. I grabbed on to the table in front of me and closed my eyes, then opened them again. The room was spinning

"Beanie, you okay?"

"Yes," I answered, feeling my lunch make its way back up my throat. "I'm fine," but I knew what had overtaken me yet again. I ran upstairs to the bathroom, where I stayed for a good long time.

"Just something I ate," I reassured Phoebe, who had positioned herself right outside the door, something I resented. After all, sometimes a girl needs her privacy. "Edwin's calamari with basil must have disagreed with me. Maybe I got a bad piece."

But I knew, in my heart of hearts, that it wasn't a bad piece of calamari that had made me ill. Instead, something rotten was growing way down inside me and, no matter what I told myself, I was having trouble keeping it down.

CHAPTER SIXTEEN

I absolutely couldn't have guessed what happened next. If you've ever tried to sell something on Craigslist, you know that it isn't as easy as it seems. Willis and I once wanted to make some cash by getting rid of an old dinghy, and it was a whole two weeks before we got a single bite. Finally, some old fogy called and asked if the boat had a mast and a motor. That was the end of that. We still have that dinghy chained up out back.

So when someone called the very day after I posted Honey's ad, I wasn't in the least prepared. I couldn't believe my luck, and at the same time, I wished I'd had another day or two before having to move on so quickly to the next step of my plan. It's one thing to think about doing something and another to actually make it happen.

A gruff voice was on the other end of the phone. "This Spike the dogman?"

"Yes, I'm Spike the dog man." I knew it was important that I sounded as professional as possible.

"Good. This is Sam. I'm a dogman too and just saw your ad about the champion."

I was confused. Who was the dog man, me or him?

"Where'd you get the mastiff?"

"From a breeder in Italy." For some reason, I thought it important to disguise my voice and covered the phone receiver with a dishcloth, the way I'd seen in a spy movie once. This way, Sam the dog man would think I was an adult. "She's very big and strong and her ancestors were real good fighters too."

"Got a receipt?"

"Yes," I lied. "And papers with her bloodlines." I had no idea where the receipt or papers were but could worry about that later.

"Never mind that, anyway," he said quickly. "I'm not planning to use her for the main event. Just to get the pits fired up. Mastiffs can't usually cut it; they're too slow and lazy."

It did seem that Sam had Honey's number. "Slow and lazy" fit her to a T. I figured that he must be pretty knowledgeable about the breed, although I didn't understand what a fire in a pit had to do with anything.

"Does she weigh over one fifty?"

"Yes, over one fifty." I didn't know what Honey weighed and couldn't imagine trying to put her on a scale. "And she's real easy to keep—we just keep her chained outside during the day."

"So she's been through the keep?"

It seemed that Sam hadn't heard me correctly when I'd said Honey was easy to keep, but I figured it was best just to let it go, instead of correcting him. I had the feeling that he wasn't the type who really wanted to chat on the phone for very long. "Yep," I responded.

"Won any in the show?" he asked.

"Yes, she won in the show." I thought that's what Phoebe had told me.

"Used to the springboard?"

I was beginning to feel flustered. "Yes," I said, figuring this would be the safest answer. I sure didn't want the man on the phone to know I had no idea what a springboard was. Maybe some kind of diving board for large dogs?

"No health problems? Open wounds?"

"No!" Open wounds?! Phoebe would never put up with that. She'd have Honey all bandaged up with iodine if even a paw had been scratched.

"What say I give you a grand? No receipt or papers. Cash free and clear."

I wasn't exactly sure what a grand was, so I just repeated what I'd written in the ad: "Three thousand, please."

"Fifteen hundred. Tops."

It took me a minute to remember that fifteen hundred meant one thousand, five hundred dollars. Half the three thousand I'd asked for. But I was desperate and figured that that would still pay for Willis's bail and Phoebe's puppy. "Okay," I said, "but I need it in cash."

"We don't exactly use personal checks, buddy. You sure you're on the level?"

It was clear to me that Sam the dog man was getting antsy, although I wasn't sure exactly why. "Yes, no. I am a dog man, I promise. And I don't use checks either, of course not. Cash is king where I come from."

"You better be on the up and up. I don't mess around. Just have the mastiff ready and we'll make a deal. I can get the dog a week from Tuesday."

Since the man was from off island, he suggested that I bring Honey to the Rock Haven dock and we could meet there for the purchase after the last ferry of the day was to arrive on island.

"Dogs are allowed on the ferry," I assured him, "and you don't even have to buy her a ticket. But please make sure you have some cranberry juice or water so she doesn't get dehydrated, and a little snack too. She likes to have something to eat every thirty minutes, preferably blueberries or even blackberries."

Silence for a minute or two. Both of my wrists started itching.

And then, finally a snarl from the other end of the phone: "How old are you anyway? You better not be—"

"I'm eighteen," I interrupted quickly, immediately understanding the error of my ways. Cranberry juice and blueberries? The guy must have thought I was an idiot. "Sorry about that, just joking."

"Listen, kid"—the man's voice dropped—"quit the jokes and don't waste my time. Just be there at the dock at ten thirty p.m., June twenty-first. It'll be dark, so easy to do our business without anyone seeing. I'll find you and the mastiff, so sit tight, but we're gonna have to make the transaction under cover. No trouble, okay? Nobody wants any trouble. There's a convention coming up next month and I'm short a dog for my two champions. They could use some new blood to keep them on their toes."

I thought it might be nice for Honey to attend a dog convention and meet some other nice dogs. At least she wouldn't be lonely.

When I hung up the phone, I was surprised to feel my stomach knot and my heart shrink to the size of an olive pit. *I should be happy*, I thought to myself. Why didn't I feel happy? After all, in only eight days, I'd have the money I needed to get Willis out of jail. But instead of being relieved, my inside organs shriveled, all black and charred. I closed my eyes and leaned back. For a minute, I thought I might get sick. The linoleum floor in my very own house started to float up, down, and I recognized what I never wanted to feel ever again.

Vertigo.

And then I puked all over the kitchen floor.

By the time my mother came home after work, I had cleaned up the floor and was lying down in my bedroom, minding my own business. Willis's bed was still unmade, as if he'd just left for school in a hurry, the way he always did, his pile of books and pillow still on the floor. I wondered if they gave him a pillow in jail.

"What's wrong, Bean?" my mother asked, even before setting one foot through my door.

"Nothing. Why does there always have to be something wrong?"

She was still wearing her dark green Stop & Shop shirt, the one with a little tear in one shoulder seam. The material buckled there, revealing a tiny dot of white. My mother was always real pale, even in the summer.

"Well, because it's only six thirty and you're already in bed."

"I'm not in bed. I'm just lying *on* my bed."

"Bean." My mother leaned over and brushed a strand of hair out of my eyes, then sat down beside me. Her own hair, dusted with silver, was pulled back with a rubber band in her usual loose ponytail and her eyes looked tired. I could always tell when my mother was beat; her whole upper body slumped forward, and the brown of her hazel eyes overtook the green. When she was feeling good or happy, it would be just the opposite. Green flooded the brown.

Neither of us spoke for a moment, then: "Are you fretting about your brother? I know it's been hard on you, Bean. Hard on me too. I've even been having trouble at work, snapping at everyone. Yesterday I got written up for being rude to customers, can you believe it? After all those years at the store without a spot on my record? But it is what it is and nothing to be done about it now."

I felt bad that my mother had gotten written up at work, but it just didn't seem that important considering what Willis was going through. And no one had really even bothered to keep me in the know about how he was doing or if there was any news about the court date. "So, is all that stuff about his court date the same?" I asked her. "Did you find out anything new? Anything changed? Do we know how long Willis will have to stay locked up?"

If there was any chance that Willis's court date was moved up, he'd get out of jail sooner and I wouldn't have to worry about selling Honey and going through with my brilliant but difficult plan.

"Not really sure exactly how long," my mother responded in a low voice, looking irritated. "Remember, Bean, Sheriff Cobbs said something about the state having two or three months before anything official is scheduled. We'll just have to wait and see."

I thought carefully for a minute. Even with almost three weeks having passed already and another one until I got the bail cash from Sam, I could still save Willis from another month of jail. Maybe even more.

I checked the numbers in my head once, then twice. Yes, if all things went as planned, I would be able to rescue my brother from at least a good thirty days of being locked up. Not too shabby, maybe even pretty good. Of course, better if I had the money right away so he could be freed immediately, but if that wasn't possible, saving him from almost month of prison was still okay. On the other hand, imagining my brother for just one more minute behind bars made my heart sink.

I'd hoped my mother would have news that Willis would be out even sooner, and would let Phoebe keep her dog, but now I knew that she didn't and I wasn't going to have a choice. I would have to go through with my plan.

"Isn't there anything we can do right now? Anything at all?"

"Nothing I can figure."

"Well, there has to be something." I felt the twist in my stomach return. "Maybe we could find him an attorney, some big hotshot from off island or something. Someone from Boston or New York, who wants to take the case for free. Why can't we do that? Why can't we be there for Willis now that he needs our help? Why does he have to stay in jail for making one little mistake? And why won't you take me to see him?" I had to stop talking because my voice started to break.

Of course I knew in my heart of hearts that it wasn't a question of one little mistake. I understood that, but at the same time, I was mad. Mad at my mother, mad at the sheriff, mad at Willis, and mad at myself for making a deal to sell Honey to the crabby dog man. It wasn't right; it wasn't fair, not fair at all.

And it made me even angrier to think that if we only had more money, Willis would already be free on bail. How was it that people with big bucks could get out of jail anytime they wanted and my brother couldn't? There had to be a better way to punish those who screwed up every once in a while. A fairer way. A way that had the same rules for all, rich or poor. My mother was a hard worker, and it wasn't her fault that we didn't have any money to spare. I knew that but still . . .

My mother turned away for a moment, and I could see her shoulders tremble. The last thing I wanted to do was make her sad, but sometimes when I got angry, I just couldn't help taking it out on her. I knew that the situation wasn't her fault, but I still wanted her to feel what I felt. Hurting my mother was wrong, but I didn't want to be hurt either.

And I couldn't, for the life of me, understand why she wouldn't try everything in her power to at least visit Willis at the jail. I knew she had long work hours, and I understood that we needed every cent from her Stop & Shop check, and yet going to visit my brother just seemed more important than any of that. While my mother had never been exactly the touchy-feely type, the kind of mom who smothered you with kisses all the time or who left you little surprise notes with your school lunch, I knew that she loved my brother and me. And Willis had always been her joy, the son who had gotten perfect grades and would go on to do great things, so I felt pretty confused about her attitude. I guess she was just disappointed, not only about Willis, but about my whole family and a bunch of other things too.

I'd once had the word *defeated* on my vocabulary list from school. When I asked my mother what that meant, she smiled kinda sadly and looked down at her chapped hands. "Defeated means being at the end of your rope, Bean. It means being worn down, beaten down by life."

So I figured that might be just how my mother was feeling now. Maybe she was too worn down by life to go see her only son in jail. Maybe she was defeated and had given up on Willis—I wasn't really sure. But I was certain about one thing and no one would ever change my mind: I'd never give up on my brother and I'd never be defeated by my own life.

When my mother turned toward me again, her thin lips were squeezed tightly together, and the brown in her eyes had completely overtaken the green. She swiped my forehead with a barely-there kiss and left the room without another word.

CHAPTER SEVENTEEN

The next morning, I hung around my room for a while instead of dashing over to see Phoebe as usual. Although I was eager to tell her about Honey's sale, I was also dreading it. Honey really wasn't that bad of a dog after all, and I worried that Sam the dog man didn't sound that nice. What if he ended up being mean to her or got mad when she shook her head in a tornado of slobber? What if he made her eat regular dog food instead of the delicacies Phoebe prepared?

And if I was concerned about the sale, I was pretty sure Phoebe would be even more upset. But I couldn't let her change her mind after I'd already sealed the deal. Then Willis would have to stay in jail, and Sam the dog man didn't sound like someone you'd want to mess with.

But before I could even finish getting dressed, the phone rang. *What's going on?* I thought to myself. *Someone else to buy Honey? There must be a shortage of Neapolitan mastiffs in Massachusetts.*

It was Phoebe herself on the phone.

"Beanie!" She sounded frantic, her voice a few pitches higher than usual. "Emergency. You have to come over right now. Please come over. I really need your help!"

My first thought was that she'd hurt herself or Edwin had finally snapped and was holding her hostage on Beach Bluff's widow's walk.

"What's wrong, Phoebe?" I felt panic rising in my throat, but knew I needed to keep calm. "What's going on? Are you okay?"

"Can't talk." Her voice dropped to a whisper. "Don't want Edwin to hear. Just come over now. I'm in my bedroom."

And then the phone went dead.

Luckily, I only had to throw on my jeans and sneakers and was out the door in one minute flat. It was one of Rock Haven's stormy summer days and the rain pelted my face as I ran. Each time I made a bit of progress forward, I was pushed back by an angry slap of warm, humid wind—it felt as though I would absolutely never make it to Beach Bluff to rescue Phoebe.

When I finally got there, I saw that the double front door had blown open and someone had tied up Honey to the front porch with a shallow bowl of blueberries floating in a few inches of cranberry juice. Her favorite treat. But who could have led her from outside all the way up the steps to the covered porch? Honey looked up at me mournfully for a second, then dunked her gigantic head back in the bowl. But there was not a second to lose, no time to think about her or anything else. I had to rescue my friend.

The old house's immense carved wooden stairway seemed endless, and I tried to take the stairs two by two, falling once or twice. I wanted to call out to Phoebe and let her know I'd be there to help in just a few seconds, but remembered what she said on the phone about not wanting Edwin to hear. Running down the second floor's long, dark hallway, I tripped on a small throw rug, skinning my elbow and chin. *Hang in*, I thought to myself. *Just hang in and breathe.*

The door to Phoebe's room was cracked open, and when I peered inside to prepare myself for whatever was to come my way, I stopped breathing.

Phoebe was curled up on the floor and a large man was standing over her, a carving knife in one hand.

My worst nightmare. I couldn't believe my own eyes.

"Leave her alone!" I screamed, throwing myself into the room. "If you touch one hair on her head, you'll be sorry! Back off now!" My voice sounded like was coming from someone else, from somewhere else, and I heard it crack like a little kid's. "I have a weapon!"

"Beanie!" Phoebe yelled. "Don't . . ."

And then the man spun around so quickly that my eyes stung. It didn't take me more than a minute to see that he was wearing an apron that said *Don't Mess with the Cook.*

CHAPTER EIGHTEEN

Edwin smirked when he saw me, the knife glinting in his hand. Pushing him out of my way, I dropped to the floor and put my arms around Phoebe. "Are you okay? What did he do to you? Are you okay?"

"Careful, Beanie, you'll hurt them. Yes, I'm fine. He didn't do anything. Just be really, really careful."

Pulling away, I saw that Phoebe was cradling a fuzzy yellow blanket in her lap. A blanket that started to move. Phoebe giggled. I noticed that she was wearing a crinkly petticoat as a skirt and that it made a squeaking sound when she shifted in place.

"Look, Beanie, kittens. We found three sweet kittens in my bedroom wall. Three babies." And smack dab in the middle of the yellow blanket, a tiny black paw popped up and then two more and then a little white-and-black kitten face. Then two more mini-faces. They all mewed together and licked one another's flat, identical spotted noses.

A large, jagged hole in the wall behind Phoebe took me by surprise. It looked as though someone had hacked it open, leaving a mess of drywall all over the floor. As if on cue, a cloud of dust floated toward us and I coughed.

Phoebe nodded. "Edwin did that, made the hole in the

wall. I thought I heard the voices this morning and didn't know what to do. That's when I called you. But I guess Edwin overheard."

Of course he did.

"Anyway, we didn't have any tools, so he cut through the wall with a knife to rescue the kittens. Good thing that Edwin knew exactly what the voices were and what to do or I don't know what would have happened. Poor babies."

So Phoebe and I weren't going crazy and Beach Bluff wasn't haunted, after all. What we'd been hearing was just the cry of three abandoned furballs stuck in the wall with no way to escape. I didn't know whether to smile with relief or shake my head at their predicament. So I did both.

I looked at Edwin, who was leaning over to brush the drywall dust off his legs and precious fleece slippers. I saw that his bun had come loose and stray strands of red hair stuck to his cheeks. He looked up, and for a minute, his eyes were soft. All of a sudden, Phoebe's nanny looked like someone else, someone I really didn't know.

Edwin wiped the perspiration off his forehead with the back of one arm, the carving knife still in his hand.

"Lucky this room has drywall instead of plaster. Unusual for such an ancient house. But these kittens look okay to me; guess their mother had been nursing them for a good bit, although there's sure no sign of her now."

"But where did she go, the mama cat?" Phoebe's voice was muffled, her face dipped in fur.

Edwin shrugged. "Who knows. Sometimes the mother heads out for food and never finds her way back. Or sometimes she'll reject the litter if she doesn't know how to care for it. Some mother cats are like that; they just aren't naturally maternal and wander away. Unusual, but it can happen in the animal world."

No one said anything for a minute.

"I grew up on a farm with a bunch of animals, including cats," Edwin explained, as if we'd asked, "and know that kittens have to be kept warm and fed or they won't survive. So you better get on the job and figure out how to keep them safe. Lunch will be late today, children, but it should be ready by half past noon. Please make sure that you're washed up, and not a single grimy feline will be allowed at the table."

While the three kittens didn't join us at the table during lunch, Phoebe and I brought them downstairs to the kitchen to get some milk. Naturally, the only kinds in the refrigerator were almond and soy, but Edwin reluctantly produced a small container of cream that we poured into a tiny, flowered china bowl.

"What should we name them?" asked Phoebe as we set down the bowl.

I shrugged. Naming the kittens was the last thing on my mind since they didn't seem very interested in the cream and the smallest one really didn't look too healthy to me. I thought that they all looked pretty skinny and pathetic, despite what

Edwin had said—and who knew how long they had actually gone without food.

"I can't believe that their mother went and why she left them all alone." Phoebe looked sad for a minute and then perked up. "But it'll be fun to take care of them," she continued. "We can bring them to the vet and make sure that they get all the food and vitamins they might need. It's okay that their mother isn't around; we'll just take over for now and maybe the mom will come back when she can. And, anyway, we could get them some really cute kitty outfits. Let's order some from one of the new catalogs."

Here we go again, I thought. The kid really had a fascination with dressing up pets. And then, just as we started talking about kitten names:

BOOM.

"What on earth!" Edwin looked up from stirring something in a pot on the stove. "Haven't we had enough excitement for today?"

Boom, boom, boom.

The slow, heavy steps of something or someone. I immediately thought that maybe Sam the dog man had come to steal Honey instead of paying the fifteen hundred dollars we'd agreed upon, but then again, how could he possibly have Phoebe's address?

Maybe an escaped convict of some kind, possibly a friend of my brother or even my brother himself, or maybe an elephant gotten loose from the zoo. Of course, my brother didn't know anything about Phoebe or Beach Bluff and we didn't have a zoo in Rock Haven. Frankly, I wasn't thinking clearly at that point, my mind turning to mush. After the whirlwind of a day I'd had so far, I just figured that anything at all was possible. I was prepared for the worst. I was prepared for the best. Nothing would have surprised me.

THUMP.

Thump. Thump. Thump.

And then . . .

In she came, proud as could be, massive head held high, bluish-silverish jowls drooping almost all the way to the floor, one giant paw shuffling after another, dragging a chunky rope leash with an entire splintering porch post still attached, her enormous barrel chest pumping slowly, white drool foaming from her muzzle.

I craned my neck to see if there was some kind of parade following her, maybe a marching band . . .

She shook her head slowly, a shower of white spittle falling over us like snow. Her eyes, almost completely covered by folds and folds of wrinkled skin, seemed to flash just before she crashed to the floor. The whole house shook.

"Honey!" Phoebe exclaimed. "Honey's come inside the house!"

"Quick, grab the kittens." I knew exactly what might come next, having witnessed the tiara incident only two weeks ago.

But before any of us could make a move, all three kittens, dislodged from the cozy corner of Phoebe's lap by the rumble of the big dog's collapse, slid across the old house's slanted kitchen floor in a messy clump of fur, landing right in front of Honey's frothing, open mouth. Phoebe and I both stood up in sudden alarm. I could see Honey's supersized tongue and all her slimy fangs; each tooth looked sharp enough to cut through the plaster walls of any *ancient* house all by itself. I closed my eyes and opened them again, almost hoping that the scene in front of me would somehow just disappear. After all, it would only take one gulp for complete disaster.

Again, I thought of Phoebe's tiara; one minute there, another minute gone. So, without skipping a beat, I lunged toward Honey, prepared to fling my body between her and the three kittens. Sometimes, I can be pretty brave.

But wouldn't you know it, Phoebe stole my thunder before I could get near the big dog. "No!" she yelled in such a loud voice that I stopped in my tracks. "No, Bean. Leave Honey alone. She would never hurt anyone or anything and I want to see if the animals will be friends. You never know. Maybe they could really like each other, even though they're different species." She sat up on her knees, her white petticoat spread out on either side like wings.

Species? Give me a break. What was Phoebe talking about and why was she so sure that the kittens would be safe?

And then the most surprising thing happened, something that I would never have guessed in a million, trillion years.

The three kittens climbed up Honey's long, sagging jowls all the way to her whiskery block of a snout and then up even farther to the very top of her silver head, clutching on with their minuscule claws. The smallest kitten seemed stuck on one ear and began to mew. Then Honey sighed so heavily that all three lost their balance, tumbling down her wrinkled muzzle. And then, one by one, each kitten scooted back all the way around, wobbling in the other direction until each buried its head in the big dog's soft belly. It was the first time that I noticed a large splotch of white on Honey's chest. It looked like a permanent stain of spilled milk.

"Why aren't they moving?" It occurred to me that the kittens might suffocate. They were so small and weak while Honey was so large and strong.

"Hush," Phoebe whispered. "Just leave them alone. Can't you see that the babies like Honey and that she's making them her own?"

Nobody said anything then, but Edwin put down his spoon and sat down on the floor with Phoebe and me, the three of us watching Honey give her new babies just what they needed.

PART THREE

HONEY

CHAPTER NINETEEN

"So do you think the kittens will really be okay nursing on Honey?" I asked Phoebe the morning after Edwin had carved a gaping hole in her bedroom wall. Phoebe and I were in the exact same position on the kitchen floor as the afternoon before, staring at the spectacle of the three babies nursing on Honey's bloated belly. The two of us were in a kind of kitten daze and I felt as if I'd been hypnotized by the soft little critters, everything else wiped from my mind.

Including Willis. Including Sam the dog man. And it was kind of a relief not to think about either of them for a little while. My plan to rescue my brother was already in place, so there wasn't any point worrying until Tuesday.

"Yes, definitely," Phoebe replied. "I read all about it in one of my books last night. Female dogs can nurse other animal babies, even if they've never been pregnant."

The whole deal seemed unnatural to me, making me wonder if we should have separated the kittens and the big dog right away. Maybe we could have found a real mother cat somewhere in town and borrowed it for a while.

"But isn't it illegal?" I'd asked. "I mean, it just seems wrong." Phoebe had looked over at me then, studying my expression carefully. Her whole face was flushed with contentment, like she'd just woken up from a happy dream.

"It doesn't matter if Honey is a dog and the kittens are, well, kittens. All that matters is that they take care of each other, like they're doing now. Don't you know that about maternal instinct? Honey has a bunch of maternal instinct for our kittens."

I felt embarrassed for a moment, realizing how much older than me Phoebe could seem, despite our ages.

Edwin was busily mopping the kitchen floor, frowning every time he approached the kitten feeding frenzy or where Phoebe and I were sitting.

"Be careful," Phoebe warned him. "You don't want to scare the kittens. You should know that, since you used to have so many animals. What other pets did you have growing up on the farm, Edwin? I mean along with your cats?"

He shrugged. "My family had goats, chickens, pigs, and an Australian shepherd. Raised him from a pup."

"Wow," I piped up, suddenly interested. "What's it like in Australia, anyway?" While I didn't have any interest in anything Edwin, Australia sounded like it might be a pretty unusual place.

"Australia?" He looked up for a minute. "I don't know. Of course, there's the Bloomin' Onion, and I hear everyone calls each other *mate*."

"What's the Bloomin' Onion?"

"Haven't you ever been to the Outback Steakhouse?" Edwin

continued to mop, and I had the feeling he was getting irritated with my questioning.

"No."

"I have!" Phoebe piped up. "I've been and tasted the Bloomin' Onion too! Mother says greasy stuff is bad for you, but I ate it anyway."

"But what's it really like?" I asked Edwin again. By this time he had made his way across the kitchen and was squeezing out the mop in a green plastic bucket. It definitely seemed like Edwin was avoiding my question.

"Why all the questions about Australia?" He adjusted his apron and dried his hands on a small towel. "Are you planning a trip Down Under?" He smiled to himself, as if he'd just said something amusing. Again, I was confused.

"Aren't you from Australia? Phoebe told me that you were from Sydney, Australia."

Edwin's caterpillar eyebrows shot up his forehead like a cartoon character's. And then he started to laugh.

I'd never seen Edwin so amused and found it a bit unsettling.

"I'm from Sydney, all right, mate," he managed to say, still chuckling. "Sydney, North Dakota."

"Wait a minute!" Phoebe looked up from the kittens for a minute. "You're not from Australia at all? Not even a little bit?"

Edwin's chuckle turned into a full-blown belly laugh. "Not sure how I could be a little bit from anywhere, Phoebe," he said, wiping his eyes. "No, I'm not from Australia at all."

Then Edwin told us that he'd lived in North Dakota all his life but had to move because there weren't any good chef positions and he needed to support his family. "I have a wife and little girl back home," he said, looking sad for a minute. "I only get to see them a few times a year. I wish things were different, but it is what it is."

There was that expression again. *It is what it is.* My mother and brother said that to me all the time, and it aggravated me to no end.

Then I remembered the photograph I'd seen on Edwin's computer wallpaper of him holding a little girl on his lap. Somehow, it was hard to imagine Phoebe's nanny as a father. And it seemed odd and even sad to me that he was taking care of Phoebe all the way in Massachusetts, when he'd left his own little girl back in North Dakota. Kinda messed up, but not that different from Honey caring for the kittens and the kittens' mother somewhere else, maybe watching over a bunch of other kittens somewhere. Sometimes, the world is a pretty crazy place.

All I knew about North Dakota was that it was far away from the East Coast and the Lakota and Ojibwa Native American tribes lived there, something I learned about in school.

"Is North Dakota colder than South Dakota?" asked Phoebe.

"I suppose." Edwin's back was to us then, and he was trying to shove the mop and bucket into the kitchen's narrow broom closet. "But you really don't care about the cold weather when you're used to it and as long as you're home with your family."

• • •

"Beanie," Phoebe asked me later that day, "which kitty do you think is the cutest? I think the middle one, the one with the spot at the end of her tail."

I shrugged. All the kittens looked about the same to me. Little skinny things with a bit of flesh and fur stretched over tiny bones. "Dunno," I replied, immediately knowing that *dunno* was never going to cut it with Phoebe.

"But which one? Go over there and look. Pick one and tell me right now." So, sighing heavily, I wandered over to where Honey and the kittens were lying in a circle of drool.

Honey didn't move an inch when I approached, except for the thumping of her long tail. Slowly at first and then faster and faster until it looked like it was a helicopter propeller going round and round. If I hadn't known better, I would have thought she was going to take off in the air right then and there. One of the kittens fell off her from the movement and began to cry.

I noticed that it was Phoebe's favorite kitten, the one with the spot on the tail, and bent over to nudge it forward to start sucking again. Honey turned, perhaps to say thanks, and then bam, her head dropped down back on the floor. I looked at the second kitten; no spot on its tail but with lighter paws than the others and maybe a smidgen fatter too. The third kitten had finished nursing before the others; it opened its little mouth, still splattered with milk, yawned, and then let out such a loud cry that all four of us, Phoebe, Edwin, Honey, and

I, looked at her with concern. This kitten had three black paws and one white one. It rubbed its head against Honey's stomach, then suddenly dropped to the floor on its back and fell dead asleep. Just like that. It seemed that this particular kitten knew how to take care of herself without anyone's help.

"This one," I said, turning back to Phoebe. "I like this one best and I think her name should be Athena." I'd learned in school that Athena was the wisest of the Greek goddesses.

"Crikey," Edwin muttered. "That doesn't seem right for a little kitten."

"Athena," Phoebe whined. "No, no, I hate that name."

For some reason, Phoebe, Edwin, and I couldn't agree on the names for the kittens. Phoebe's names were always sappy, like Midnight or Shadow or Whiskers, and Edwin's were just plain foolish. Who in their right mind calls a cat Barbie or Roo? I thought Edwin was just messing with us though, since he found the Australian misunderstanding hilarious. He told us that *barbie* meant barbecue in Australia and *roo* was the word for kangaroo. He also kept calling us *mate* every chance he got. Edwin seemed to get a lot of pleasure out of teasing us, which was annoying as all get out.

For the two days after finding the kittens, things at Beach Bluff seemed different. Maybe we were all in a kind of kitten trance, finding it hard to tear away our eyes from the scene on the kitchen floor. We were each quieter then, usually speaking to

142

one another in low voices, not wanting to disturb Honey or frighten the little ones in her care. And we moved slowly, the way you do when swimming underwater, drifting around the kitchen only when necessary.

Phoebe and I were both hesitant to leave our watchful post, only changing position to sit at the table for lunch. We were also surprised to see that Edwin, quietly, carefully, began cleaning every corner of Beach Bluff so that each room gleamed. He glided around the house as if on ice skates, hardly making a sound as he dusted and polished every visible surface, and I was surprised at how such a large man could be so graceful.

While we weren't sure why Edwin had suddenly decided to spiff up Beach Bluff, I just figured it had to do with Phoebe's parents' upcoming visit. They had originally planned on arriving mid-June but had recently delayed their trip another two weeks, so I was confused about why Edwin was on such a cleaning spree. "Because of a fancy party or gala or luncheon or something real important in France, that's why my parents are coming a little late," Phoebe told me. "But just wait until you meet my mother, Beanie; she's real, real pretty and always wears pretty clothes too. She's got a whole bunch of silk dresses and high heels." Phoebe was beaming at the thought. "I wish I had hair like hers. It's wavy and has golden highlights. And my father is pretty handsome, but he's kind of short and doesn't have any hair. He used to smoke these funny, special brown cigarettes from Morocco but doesn't anymore since they're bad for you and could make you sick. Just wait until you meet them both and you'll see."

The thought of meeting Phoebe's parents made me nervous. They'd probably think that I was just some worthless island kid hanging around with their daughter and send me on my way. Not to speak of my plan to sell their dog. What if I could never come to Beach Bluff or see Phoebe ever again? What if I was banned for life?

While I had originally thought Edwin's cleaning was meant to impress the Sinclairs, Phoebe was sure that Edwin was sprucing up for the kittens. "He wants everything to be perfect for the kittens and for Honey. Sanitary. It's very important that the babies stay happy and don't get a cold or something from bacteria dirt. You know you should always, always wash your hands before touching the kittens since they're just born."

I knew that. Phoebe had told me over a hundred times.

Edwin even pulled open all the heavy window drapes and polished each pane of glass so carefully that it was hard to tell the inside from the outside. He found a bright green-and-white tablecloth with little cherries on the border in one of the butler's pantry drawers, washed and steam ironed it so when dropped over the kitchen table like a magician's cape, there wasn't a single wrinkle. I thought that the starched cotton smelled good, a scent that somehow reminded me of the beach and my mother's old checkered summer dresses from years ago.

Beach Bluff practically shone under Edwin's touch, daylight brightening every dark corner and tinting the gloomy walls with sunshine. In the evening, particularly at sunset, the entire place lit up pink and buttery yellow underneath. Phoebe would look all gauzy then, crouched over three kittens and the silver hunk of their adoptive mother, Honey.

Late on Wednesday, just as Edwin was getting ready to take Honey out for a walk, I discovered that the three kittens were missing. Phoebe and I were having our daily name-the-kitten discussions and I was trying to make an important point about how the kittens' different personalities should match their names. But when I looked over to the cardboard box where they slept when Honey was out for a walk, it was completely empty. Not a single kitten to be seen.

"Phoebe," I asked slowly. "Where are the kittens?"

"What do you mean, where are the kittens? They're in their nursery room, dummy." Phoebe liked to call the cardboard box the kittens' nursery room and I'd stopped trying to correct her.

"No, they're not."

"Go look again."

I looked again but didn't see hide nor hair of a single kitten. The box had one of Phoebe's mother's violet silk shawls folded neatly as bedding and I even looked underneath. When I turned around to report back, Phoebe was already on her hands and knees, checking every inch and corner of the floor.

"Could they have followed Honey outside?" I heard an unfamiliar note of panic in my own voice.

145

By this time, Phoebe had run out the front door and I could hear her calling, "Honey, Edwin! Here, kitty, kitty, kitty. Here, kitty, kitty. Come home. Please come on home."

I followed her to the porch and squinted. Sometimes Edwin took Honey down the block for a real walk, but he mostly just crossed the street to the bluff's edge and let her do her business right there in the small bushes and tall grasses overlooking the water.

Edwin wasn't across the street, and when we finally did spy him huffing and puffing back to the house, Honey dragging slowly behind, Phoebe started screaming, "Edwin, the kittens are gone. The kittens are gone. Look to see if they followed you. Are they behind Honey? I can't tell from here!"

He looked confused for a moment and then stopped in his tracks, a distressed expression falling over his face. Turning around faster than I've ever seen him move, he circled behind Honey, who had stopped to sniff a plastic cup blown in her path. Then Edwin shook his head slowly and pulled Honey back toward the house.

The four of us collapsed together on the porch, and I swatted angrily at a sudden swarm of mosquitoes. It seemed impossible that the kittens could have vanished just like that, one minute there and the next gone. Poor Phoebe was sobbing, her face smeared with boogers and tears; for a minute I wanted to put my arm around her and have a good cry too but couldn't quite bring myself to move. Extreme expressions of emotions were never really all that big in my family.

Edwin patted her on the head, then on the back as if trying to burp a baby, and Honey just sat there, happy as a clam, snuffling and passing clouds of gas as usual. For a minute, I almost felt angry at her for losing the kittens we had just found, but then realized that they were our responsibility as much as hers. I reached over to pat the long bridge leading to her black nose and then smoothed the fur all the way down her drooping, wrinkled cheeks. She grunted in appreciation.

And then I saw the bulges. Not again! Honey often picked up all kinds of disgusting things on her walks and stored them in her jowls to munch on later. We'd often find her chewing on assorted items later in the day: a lost toy, a tube of sunscreen, and once, someone's leather wallet. This time, the big dog had apparently picked up beach rocks or old tennis balls on her walk with Edwin because I saw that her jowls stretched even farther than usual with the weight and were swollen with some newly discovered and probably gross treasure.

"Honey," I said, getting annoyed all over again. "You'll get very sick if you keep swallowing all that stuff from the ground."

An emergency trip to the vet was not what we needed when the kittens were missing. Phoebe helped me pry open the dog's jaws while I pulled up the roof of her mouth. Edwin looked at the procedure nervously from a safe distance. Thick saliva covered my hand all the way up to my elbow. Brave individual that I was, I then slid my hand down one jowl to the very bottom where she'd stored her prize.

To my shock and surprise, I didn't retrieve a rock or old

tennis ball from Honey's jowl. What I felt there, all the way down in her dark well of slime, was something alive. I could feel something moving and a little heart beating against my palm. And then another, and another.

Three little kittens.

It turned out that Honey had been sneakier than we could have imagined. Right before it was time for her afternoon walk, she must have collected the three kittens in her jowls and carried them out the door without anyone noticing. All three were in her cheeks, safe and sound, and when I dug them out, the big girl licked each one and then nudged them into a small, soft cave in her sagging neck. She sat there for a minute, then tugged on one of my own hands, taking it into her mouth. There was a moment when I wondered if I'd ever see all five fingers again, but she just held my hand there gently for a second, never bearing down, as if considering what to do next. Then she pulled both me and my hand down to where the kittens were neatly bundled. I almost tripped over into her broad chest.

"She wants to make you one of her babies," Phoebe said, smiling. "I think Honey loves you, Beanie. She wants to take care of you too."

Why did my eyes fill up for a second? And why did I lean over to plant a big kiss on Honey's damp nose? I removed my hand from her mouth gingerly but felt the warmth of her breath all evening long.

CHAPTER TWENTY

Phoebe didn't waste any time researching the kitten-in-jowl phenomenon and told us that it wasn't all that unusual. I guess some dogs often carry their puppies in their mouths and jowls to move them from one place to another and it appeared to be completely safe. We weren't sure, however, if it was such a good idea for the kittens to travel like that all the way down the block when Honey went out for her walk, so all three of us got into the habit of checking jowls before Edwin attached her leash.

It was pretty funny, when you thought about it, each of us sticking our hands into the big dog's endless cheek, rooting around and sometimes pulling out a kitten or three. Sometimes a complete change of clothes would be needed after the procedure since our shirts would get so wet and slimy that it was impossible to wear them anymore. Luckily for me, Phoebe had an endless supply of clothing for me to borrow, but I sure wasn't going to be caught dead in one of her dopey outfits, I can tell you that. Her plain white shirts suited me just fine.

Edwin refused to do his part without wearing long blue rubber gloves and gagging throughout the procedure. Not exactly what I would have expected from someone who'd grown up on a farm. But I sure got a big kick out of watching him.

I came to see, however, that ole Edwin wasn't that bad a dude, after all. He may have been kind of odd and moody, but he probably missed his family and real home back in Sydney, North Dakota. Once, I pointed out a gaping hole at the toe of one of his grimy fleece slippers and suggested that he invest in a new pair. Something about the old things, hole in the toe and all, made me sad, although I wasn't really sure why.

But Edwin glared and told me that his wife had given them to him one Christmas, and he didn't care about the hole or what I thought, *mate*. I kinda felt bad for saying anything.

The thing was that Edwin might snap at me or give me the evil eye, but I learned that was just his way. Sometimes you just have to accept people as they are, although I wasn't always particularly good at that.

Most important was that Edwin looked after Phoebe with kindness. I could forgive him almost anything when I saw how gently he tended to her in place of her real parents, who seemed to me to be humungous stinkos.

So Edwin took care of Phoebe, Phoebe of Honey, Honey of the kittens and sometimes maybe even me. I guess Mr. Spencer was also somewhere in the mix too since Phoebe had often seen him comforting the big dog in the evenings, but I didn't know too much about that.

Maybe everyone needed to be rescued every now and then.

As we approached the fateful day I was to meet Sam the dog man, I tried to put Honey's sale out of my mind. Sam's arrival was only five short days away and yet I managed to squeeze the whole thing into a small corner of my brain just as if it really didn't exist. You can do that, if you try really hard. It's possible to lie, even to yourself.

And so I did.

But at the same time, I was spending most of my time with Phoebe, Edwin, and Honey at Beach Bluff and getting to like each one of them more and more. When my mother had finally noticed that I was coming home later and later in the afternoons, I said, "Just hanging out with some kids at the Point. You know. Nothing really all that special."

I didn't want my mother to know that I'd made a friend who lived in a bluff mansion and had her own nanny. Somehow, I still felt weird about my mother knowing that. But I did share a few stories about Honey, how the big dog was feeding the kittens, and how she would stuff them into her cheeks when she thought no one was looking.

"You're kidding!" my mother exclaimed one evening as she put the groceries away and turned to look at me. "That's the most amazing thing I've ever heard."

And so, when she sat down at the table to fold up the brown paper grocery bags, I told her all about Honey, how gigantic she was, how her jowls looked like pancakes or burnt pizza dough, and how, when she shook her head, you needed an umbrella to stay dry. Then I told my mother about how Honey knew exactly how to comfort the kittens and feed them her special milk. How wrinkles fell over her eyes in rolls and rolls of skin, and how, just the other day, she licked both of my feet at the same time with her enormous tongue, then nuzzled her nose into the space between my arm and waist, almost knocking me down.

When I was finished, my mother looked up and smiled. "Sounds like you really like that dog, Bean. I'm glad you've gotten your mind off your brother."

"Nah," I said, sort of embarrassed. "Nah, Honey's too big and too smelly. And I really don't like dogs, anyway. They're annoying and too much trouble to have around." And I certainly hadn't gotten my mind off Willis. No way.

But, that night, when I undressed and saw a drift of Honey's fur on my jeans, I found myself smiling. The fur floated off my pants, then hovered over Willis's bed, a wisp of shimmer in the shape of a halo.

So the idea of selling Honey to Sam the dog man became more and more upsetting to me, and though I continued to try not thinking about it, this got pretty hard as the awful date got closer. While I knew that my brother was more important than any dog, Honey wasn't really just any old animal you'd run into anywhere, but more like a human or at least part human. I wasn't exactly sure why, but slowly, each time that I saw her lapping her kittens with that endless pink tongue and depositing them down the long tunnel of her jowls, the more I saw her light. I don't want to sound cheesy or anything, but if you looked closely into the big dog's eyes, there would be no end to looking. Her eyes pulled my own eyes closer and closer to a twinkle of spirit inside. But it wasn't the kind of dark spirit that I used to think lurked in Beach Bluff's walls. More like one with its own warm intelligence and heartbeat.

And if you've never seen a Neapolitan mastiff like Honey give a kitten a bath, well, you really haven't lived. Honey would eyeball one particular ball of fur, her entire chunky muzzle frozen in place, not a single ripple of skin or whisker moving. Then she'd slowly nudge the kitten with her snout until she'd moved it into place, unfold her spongy tongue, and begin washing. Every once in a while the tiny critter would fly a few inches away as the endless tongue prodded, lapped, and licked but then immediately skidded back under Honey's busy mouth. You'd think that something so small, so delicate as a kitten would be terrified by this process, but it was pretty clear that every single one of Honey's tiny gang wanted nothing more than her attention. Bath or not.

I wasn't exactly sure how a cat would tend to her kittens, but Honey always seemed to know exactly what to do, calming the babies when they cried and making sure they were always comfortable, safe, and warm.

Honey, dripping with drool, creases and folds covering her whole body like a rumpled coat turned inside out, creating storms of spittle every time she shook her head, was actually a pretty unusual dog when you really thought about it. I guess you could say that she was an acquired taste.

I began to understand that selling Honey was going to be more than difficult.

But in the end, I really didn't have a choice. If I wanted to raise the cash for Willis, I'd have to go through with the plan, no matter how I felt about the big dog or selling her to Sam. Time was running out. And the first step in accepting the cards I'd been dealt, or dealt by my own self for that matter, would be talking to Phoebe again, something I dreaded and knew would be hard, even though she had already agreed to the plan. Sometimes what you think you want to do is different once it's really time to do it. Phoebe definitely wanted a little puppy and had said she was willing to sell the big dog, but in my heart of hearts, I worried that she might have changed her mind. I worried that her new interest in the kittens may have led her astray.

As predicted, the next morning, when I absolutely couldn't put it off any longer and finally worked up my nerve to tell Phoebe about the deal I made with Sam the dog man, she objected right away and then got upset. Really, really upset.

"Oh, no, we can't sell Honey now," she insisted, motioning over to where the animals were snuggled on the floor. "Honey and the kittens are a family and it's not good to break families up. How would you feel about selling your mother or your brother?" I looked up quickly. For a minute, I'd forgotten that I'd told Phoebe I had a brother. Somehow her mentioning him made me uncomfortable. "I don't need a puppy anymore, anyway. I've got the kittens instead." To my annoyance, Phoebe looked pretty pleased with herself. She was wearing white tights with a black T-shirt and had used a wad of Scotch tape to attach pointed paper ears to her bedazzled velveteen headband. Delicate black whiskers were drawn carefully on her face, Edwin's doing, since Phoebe couldn't draw a straight line.

"In tribute of the newly born," Edwin had said earlier, noticing the surprise on my face when I first saw the meticulous whiskers, "let's not forget that a chef is also an *artiste*."

"Phoebe," I pleaded. "We've talked about this. I've already made the deal to sell Honey, and believe me, it really wasn't easy. You can't change your mind now." I was tempted to tell her all about my conversation with the mysterious dog man and about my needing the money for Willis but knew better. Both would have to stay secrets. In any case, I didn't want Phoebe to be an accomplice to a crime if I were caught and things went downhill fast. And I wasn't kidding myself; selling Honey, no matter how good the motive, was wrong

"Honey can*not* leave her babies." Phoebe's right hand flew to her mouth, and she immediately started chowing down on her fingernails. Her thin wrist, all circled with scabs from mosquito bites, suddenly looked so forlorn that I felt my eyes sting. But just for a minute.

"Phoebe, you do understand that those aren't Honey's real babies, don't you?" Once I'd spoken, I immediately regretted it.

"You think I'm dumb, don't you?" Phoebe's face turned red, and the splatter of freckles across her nose and cheeks darkened. "You just think I'm a dumb little kid. Of course I know the difference between a dog and a cat. You're the dumb one, selling Honey to somebody we don't even know."

"Phoebe . . ."

"No. No way." She banged both fists on the table. One paper ear fell to the floor, and she swatted at my hand as I reached for it.

I'd never seen Phoebe so angry before. In fact, I'd never really seen her angry at all, and she was usually the first one to see the good in everything and everyone. While it wasn't a complete surprise that she was upset, her fury was over the top. Her whole face was screwed up into a ferocious knot, and even her hair seemed to tremble with rage. For a minute, I was almost scared of her.

"Look," I said softly, "let's be reasonable. You want a puppy and I could use some cash. We agreed . . ."

"Shut up." I could hardly believe my ears. "Just shut up, Beanie. I can't believe that you'd still want to go through with it. Honey isn't going anywhere, so just shut up about it. Now, I don't want to speak to you anymore, and I'm going to go read in my room. Make sure you watch the kittens unless you want to sell them too."

Phoebe stood up, crossed her arms, and looked away. "Maybe I'll want to hang out with you tomorrow, Beanie," she spat, "but maybe I won't." And then with one paper ear flopping over her sparkly headband, she kicked the chair beside her, just for emphasis, and stomped upstairs.

I sighed and slumped over the table. It looked like I was on my own, no older brother, no friend in sight.

In the heat of the moment, Phoebe had left behind her black-and-white composition book, and it sat there on the table, calling my name, despite the *keep out* instructions. Slowly, as if happening upon the book by mistake, I reached out my hand and opened the cover. My fingers riffled through the pages idly, finally landing on a drawing with a few words scrawled underneath. Phoebe had drawn a pen-and-ink picture of two people standing next to a little girl. Underneath, in my friend's crooked handwriting, was a small list numbered 1 through 5.

Things I want:
1. Shiny hair like my mother's
2. My own TV
3. To go to a different school
4. To go on trips with mother and father
5. To have one, same home forever and ever

I closed the notebook quickly. I really didn't want to see more. Then the tiniest cry came from one of the kittens. I swiveled around to make sure everything was all right and counted: one, two, three. All accounted for and now snuggling in between Honey's bulky front paws. As if noticing that I was looking, the big dog raised her head and returned my gaze. It wasn't easy to find her eyes under all that muddle of wrinkled flesh, but when she blinked, I saw the delicate half-moons of pink underneath. She cocked her head to one side and then moaned softly. The kittens readjusted their positions and then settled down again. I walked over to Honey, without even understanding exactly why, and put my hand on her glossy dome of a head. She nudged toward me until I was holding her entire warm muzzle in my own two hands.

Walking home, I couldn't stop thinking about Honey and the kittens. I was also feeling pretty crummy about upsetting Phoebe, especially after snooping in her notebook and seeing the fifth item in the Things I Want List. Now I had to go and make her feel even worse by selling her own dog.

I knew that we'd both agreed to sell the big dog, but I also knew that I'd bribed my friend with the idea of a puppy. Of course, the sale was for the greater good—getting the money needed for bail—but somehow, the whole thing just didn't feel right. In fact, the difference between right and wrong was getting harder and harder to figure.

I scratched the three hives under my left arm. The whole hive deal was driving me crazy. It felt like I'd been scratching nonstop since my birthday. Well, maybe since before my birthday, long before. Maybe since my father vanished into thin air.

It was a super-foggy early afternoon, difficult to see even a few steps ahead, the lighthouse foghorns in rare form, sending out their husky warnings every few minutes. Ocean and shore were blurred, both swallowed up by thick white mist, and I started to feel lightheaded, sort of seasick although on dry land. I tried to imagine what it would be like to be lost at sea in this kind of weather—only the foghorns to alert about dangers ahead. Lighthouses and foghorns seemed old-fashioned with all the new technologies around. And yet, still comforting. I wasn't sure why, but definitely comforting.

As I continued to stumble home, I kept thinking about the dog man and how mean he'd sounded on the phone. Why hadn't I spoken up and asked him more questions about Honey's new home? Phoebe had been right; the least I could have done was gotten information about Honey's future. I hated to think of her treated badly, with any disrespect. What if she'd be expected to go on long walks or even jogging? Honey had very particular habits and exercising wasn't one of them.

I was halfway home when I felt something sting one foot, but when I took off my sneaker, I saw it was only a fragment of seashell, ribbed on the outside but with a speck of glitter inside. Willis told me once me that the gleaming seashells sold to tourists in the town shops weren't collected on the beach but taken from living animals, mollusks.

"What are mollusks?" I'd asked.

"Just sea critters with shells. You know, slugs, snails, squid."
He'd smiled. "All the *S* creatures but others too. Those shells
on the beach come from mollusks that have already died, but
those shiny shop seashells are made by killing the mollusk
when it's still alive."

My foot still throbbed, so I bent down to check out the
damage. Just a few specks of blood on one corner of my sole.
The gash was small, but I could also see it was deep. I slipped
my sneaker back on, continuing to limp along slowly.

I knew from experience that, no matter how little, these
were the kinds of wounds that kept hurting and took forever to
heal. It might be a long time until I made it all the way back
home. Maybe better to turn around and hash it all out with
Phoebe, maybe even tell her the whole truth. Considering her
epic meltdown, I wasn't looking forward to seeing her again, but
there really wasn't anything else to be done. The kid might have
been younger and smaller than me, but she sure knew how to
keep me in line. Well, maybe not actually keep me in line, but
do her very best. Unfortunately for Phoebe, her best just wasn't
good enough and there was no way I was going to give up on my
plan. Although my plan seemed to be getting more difficult day
by day.

But maybe, just maybe, Phoebe had cooled down a bit and
remembered how much she wanted that little puppy. I wasn't
exactly forcing her to sell Honey, was I? It had been a mutual
decision when you really thought about it. And I had planned

to give her five hundred dollars, keeping the thousand dollars needed for Willis's bail. So taking a deep breath, I turned around and started to limp slowly back to the bluff.

Phoebe met me at Beach Bluff's front door, as if she expected my return, with her thin arms crossed over her chest and a scowl on her face. Her hair was slicked back off her face in a tight, neat ponytail, highlighting her round gray eyes and emphasizing her dark mood. Even her freckles looked angry; they seemed to have multiplied like an army of frenzied ants.

Phoebe was definitely still furious and ready to take me on all over again. Not exactly a surprise, but a girl could hope.

"Who invited you over?" She looked me up and down, from head to toe, and then frowned.

"Come on, Phoebe, don't be like that. Can I come in? I've really got to tell you something. I've got an idea." I'd never seen my friend look so glum; her mouth was usually stretched into a wide, goofy smile. "Everything okay?"

"What'd you care? You sold Honey and now she has to go far away. Why didn't you tell me that you were still planning to get rid of my dog? And how are her babies going to eat if Honey's gone? If they get sick and die, it'll all be your fault." She plopped down on the porch steps and put her head down in her arms.

"Mr. and Mrs. Sinclair's trip to the island has been delayed again, and Phoebe's quite distressed." On cue, Edwin appeared on the porch without a sound, then handed me a bowl of clementines. "These might give you both a lift." And before I could say thank you, he had already closed the front door.

"They won't be here until July," Phoebe said, grabbing one clementine in each hand. "Mother said that they were going to come in June and now they won't. That stinks. And thanks to you, Honey won't be here either. And you don't even know where she's going. You stink too."

"But that was our plan, remember? You agreed so that we could get you a little puppy to carry around in a basket." I found myself whining and almost wishing that I'd gone home instead of turning back. The thought of hiding out in my room all day under the covers was suddenly appealing. "That was our plan from the beginning." I could see that she wasn't in any mood to hear me out. "Look," I continued, "I'm sorry about your parents but I have an idea that might make you feel better. Would it cheer you up if I found out exactly where Honey will be going and something about her new home? Maybe we could even visit her there. And maybe she could even come here for overnights with you at Beach Bluff. How does that sound? How about that?"

"Beanie, that won't happen and you know it. You're just trying to tell me a story so I won't be mad."

The kid was smart, I'd give her that, but it bothered me to see her upset.

For some reason it was very important to me that Phoebe agreed as well as understood. Maybe because I didn't know

162

how I could actually go through with selling the big dog all by myself and needed her on my side. Not only for friendly support but also because I really didn't want to commit the crime of kidnapping Honey. If Phoebe agreed, well, then we'd be selling her dog. That seemed like a lot less wrong. "I'll get in touch with the man who wants to buy her again and maybe you could talk to him on the phone and ask all the questions you want. And if you decide that you really still don't want to sell Honey, we won't."

What was I saying? How in the world would I contact Sam and, obviously, I needed to go through with the sale. I made a mental note to add *liar* to my list of character defects.

"So we won't sell her unless I say it's okay?"

"Right."

"And she'll only go to the nicest family."

"Yes, only to a nice family."

"A family with puppies and kittens."

"Phoebe!" She was really pushing it.

"But I get to give the okay."

"Yes. I've already said that."

"Promise?"

"Promise."

Her head popped up. I could see that she'd already split one clementine open, and its juice squirted me in the eye. She aimed for the other eye and squirted me again. Then, thank goodness, she smiled.

But I knew that I'd made a deal with the devil and was probably going straight to hell. All the way *Down Under*, so to speak. And I had to bite my lip to keep nausea at bay. Vertigo was circling and ready to pounce, but this time, it would have to wait until I left Beach Bluff and was out of Phoebe's sight.

CHAPTER TWENTY-ONE

Once, Willis had thought about researching our father online just to find out exactly where he was and what he was up to. After all, we'd barely heard from him and really didn't even know where he was living. But after mulling it over for a while, my brother ended up changing his mind.

"Guess we just should let it go, Bean," he'd said to me, swatting me on the head, the way he always did. "I guess it is what it is. Some things are better left alone." And then my brother had grabbed me in a half nelson, until we both hit the ground.

I realized now, after all that time, that both Willis and my mother used the same line: "It is what it is."

But maybe it wasn't enough, after all, to just accept things as they were and maybe, instead of always accepting "it is what it is," we shouldn't be satisfied until it was what it could be.

And so, after promising Phoebe that I'd get more information on Honey's new owner, I found myself on Saturday morning back in front of the computer at the Rock Haven Public Library. The library was pretty empty, except for a few tourists looking at the sepia historical photographs of the island that lined the walls. Mr. Costa, the children's librarian, smiled at me as I passed his cubicle and, to my irritation, got up and followed me over to the computer.

"You must have a pretty interesting personal project that you're working on, Bean, since school's out. Didn't I just see you in here in the library the other day?" Mr. Costa bent over so he could whisper in my ear. His breath smelled sharp, like he'd just eaten a garlic sandwich or something, even though I wasn't sure that there was such a thing. I liked Mr. Costa all right, he was pretty nice, and I was good friends with all his sons—who often fished with me at the annual September Bluefish Derby, but I sure wished he hadn't bent so close right then.

"Yep," I replied, happy that I hadn't logged on yet. It would be bad news if anyone found out what I was up to.

"Anything I can help you with?"

I shook my head, trying to nudge my chair away from him without being obvious and seeming rude. An army of garlic molecules was invading my nostrils and I sneezed.

"We haven't seen you around much this summer, Bean— stop by the house when the boys get back from Rhode Island."

Luckily, Mr. Costa ambled over to his desk then, and became distracted by some book he was reading. I figured it could be pretty dull if you were a children's librarian during the summer. Quickly turning my attention back to the computer and logging on, I entered Sam the dog man's information. Nothing. Of course, I didn't have any real information on him in the first place and couldn't imagine why I'd thought that typing in four words—*Sam the dog man*—would have any result at all. If only I'd gotten his last name or learned where he lived. Pretty dumb that I hadn't and just accepted everything he said like a dope. But I had a hunch that Sam wasn't really that eager to give out too much personal stuff, anyway.

Next, I just entered *dog man*. Nada.

It looked like I wasn't going to find anything worthwhile and couldn't shake a feeling of dread along with a familiar itching on both wrists. I'd made a deal to sell Honey, so I would have to go through with it, but I wished I'd asked more questions about where the dog was going, where she'd be living, and exactly how she'd be taken care of. Then I remembered a few confusing words Sam had mentioned on the phone. Maybe I'd get a better idea about Honey's future if I found out what they meant. I'd been pretty nervous at the time and hadn't wanted to sound like a dweeb by asking too much, but I realized now that it was a mistake to have stayed completely silent. What was it that Sam mentioned that I hadn't understood? I racked my brain. Something about *the keep* and a *springboard*.

If you bring up Google on the computer and type *the keep*, this is what you get:

1. Reviews of the horror film *The Keep*
2. Information about a bar and brasserie named *The Keep* (BTW, brasserie apparently has nothing to do with bras)
3. Interviews with actors from the film *The Keep*

Realizing that I was going nowhere fast, I decided to give up and try researching *springboard*. Here's what I found:

1. Information about an online course called Springboard to Success
2. Information about a data entry system called Springboard Systems
3. Information about a diving board— Springboards for Your Outdoor Pool

Awesome.

Fascinating as all this was, none of it had anything to do with dogs, or dog men for that matter. What in the heck was I going to tell Phoebe after just assuring her that I could find out a bunch more about Honey's new home, and making sure that she had visiting privileges there? And what was I going to tell myself after selling the big dog while knowing absolutely nothing about her new owner? What kind of person does that? The kind who is selfish and doesn't think ahead.

Just as I was about to give up, I had another thought. What if I typed in *dog man*, *the keep*, and *springboard* all together?

Still nothing.

So in a last-ditch attempt, I typed *dog convention* and *springboard* just to mix things up a bit.

Scrolling down the page of results, I was amazed at how many dog conventions were held all over the country. But on closer examination, most just seemed to be companies trying to sell new products, like dog food or dog medicine, although I did see a service dog convention to be held in Santa Fe, New Mexico, and one for "serious" canine behavior problems in Houston, Texas.

It wasn't until the bottom of the second page when I came across an article that was so disturbing that I had to immediately close it down.

I sat, stunned, at the library's computer desk, too upset to move. And then, taking a deep breath, logged on again and opened up the page that I'd just left.

Eighteen Dogs Seized

Junction, Tennessee—Eighteen dogs were removed from a dogfighting operation in Cheatham County, Tennessee, after a concerned citizen tipped off the Animal Rescue Corp. Upon arriving at the scene, the rescuers found eighteen dogs, some crowded in cages and others on short chains. All of the dogs needed immediate medical attention and none had access to water or food. Investigators also said that dogfighting paraphernalia such as treadmills and springboards were found.

"Dogfighting is a felony, and we take this very seriously," said County Sheriff Dan Weeps. "We are determined to prosecute all involved to the full extent of the law."

It had to be a coincidence. Our Honey wasn't going to be used for dogfighting; it just wasn't possible.

And then:

Eleven Charged in Dogfighting Crime

Troy, New York—Federal agents seized sixty-eight dogs after locating a mortally wounded American pit bull at the site of a suspected dogfighting operation in rural New York. Agents searched the scene and found over sixty German shepherds and pit bulls with their chains staked to the ground. Agents also reported that half the dogs had cuts on their faces and that many were pregnant.

In a statement, US Attorney Mary Ogden said, "Dogfighting is barbaric and has no place in a civilized society." Six New York and five New Jersey men have been charged in conjunction with this crime. Purveyors of dogfighting operations, known as dog men, often keep animals in isolated areas and train them to become as ferocious as possible. US Attorney Ogden stated that she will not tolerate animal cruelty in any form and has a zero-tolerance policy on this issue.

I felt sick to my stomach and waited for vertigo to kick in, since it usually started with nausea. Thankfully, the library walls didn't whirl and the floor didn't tilt up or down; in fact, I felt oddly clearheaded.

All of my faculties were needed now—this was serious business and I wasn't going to let down Honey, no matter what. Here was a time when *it is what it is* didn't even begin to cut it. This was my opportunity to speak out and let my voice be heard.

Continuing to scroll through a few more articles, I learned that illegal, harmful drugs are often given to the animals in order to make them stronger and meaner; I learned that lots of dogs are killed in these fights, and that some are even used as bait. And then I came upon another article, one that warned about how many underground dogfighting groups there were in this country, run by criminals known as dogmen, and included a definition of terms, secret code words used by these men so as to avoid detection by the authorities. I saw that *the keep* meant a rigorous training program in preparation for fighting and that springboards and treadmills were often used to get the animals into shape. I read that dogs that had killed were called champions and grand champions, and that a dog convention wasn't a display of products or an opportunity for improving pet behavior, but a large meeting of the dogmen, gamblers who made their money by betting on which dog would be dead first.

I finished reading and logged off the computer. Standing up, I felt a rush of icy fury and started to shiver as if just coming out of frigid ocean water on Hermit Beach. People were actually making money by torturing innocent animals and then having the dogs kill one another?

My heart tightened into a fist, pumping cold anger through

my veins. Maybe I couldn't bring my father back or be sure about rescuing Willis right there and then, but I would do something about those creeps who hurt animals. In that moment, I became taller, older, stronger. My own power was dizzying, but it was a very different kind of dizzy than from the dreaded vertigo.

My feet were firmly planted on solid ground.

I knew exactly what I had to do. I would find a way to save as many dogs in danger as I could and make sure that no more animals would be harmed.

And yet I really wasn't quite sure how to do it.

Phoebe was always telling me that I saw the worst in most everything and everyone instead of the good. "You don't like a million things," she told me once after I'd complained about having to wait in line at Coastal now that it was tourist season. She couldn't understand why I hadn't liked Honey and Edwin in the beginning, why I'd found Beach Bluff so creepy, why I didn't appreciate all the books she loved, or any books for that matter, why I hated school, and why I so resented summer visitors to the island, making fun of them at every chance possible. She couldn't figure out why I wore the same boring tee and jeans every day (although I did alternate T-shirts) or why I didn't enjoy our sessions styling Honey with her mother's wardrobe. Sometimes Phoebe would look at me with such a puzzled expression that I could tell she had no understanding of where I was coming from or why.

But I knew that she also liked and maybe even admired me. And I guess together we made a pretty good team.

Of course, Phoebe also had no inkling that my father had abandoned us off island and that my brother was sitting in jail. She didn't know that my mother had to work so hard that I barely saw her and she was too tired to do much of anything when I did. It wasn't as though I felt sorry for myself all the time and went around moping. But I did see things as they really were and not just as I wanted them to be. And now I was grateful for that.

"We aren't selling Honey," I informed Phoebe late that very afternoon. Then, under my breath: *"But I'm sure going to rattle some cages."*

And that's all I told her. I'd made up my mind that sharing more would be a mistake. I didn't want Phoebe to know what Sam had planned for Honey or anything about dogfighting. She was only two years younger than me; in some ways, she seemed much older and in other ways, much younger, and I couldn't imagine her reaction if I reported that there were criminals planning the torture of any dog, no less Honey. She wouldn't be able to handle it.

"So Honey gets to stay here where she belongs?" Phoebe was sitting cross-legged on the kitchen floor, holding her favorite kitten. "Definitely?"

Definitely.

I had to admit that it made me feel pretty good to see

Phoebe so happy when I told her that selling Honey was a no-go. Her eyes lit up all spangled, and her smile spread across her face like nobody's business. And I suddenly noticed that she wasn't quite so pale and thin as she used to be—I figured Edwin's meals and the island's sun had a good effect. There was a splash of suntan over her narrow shoulders and her cheeks had plumped up golden. I also was glad to see that her fingernails weren't quite as ragged as they were when I first met her, although she still gnawed on them when something made her mad or nervous. And while she continued to dress up in wild outfits, I thought she almost looked . . . well, I thought she almost looked pretty nice in some of them. Today's denim capri pants paired with a long, striped silk blouse and yellow vinyl belt from her mother's trunk just didn't happen to be one of them. I think it might have been the white knee socks that killed the deal.

"Yup." I smiled at Phoebe. "It turned out that the guy who wanted to buy her changed his mind."

"Why?"

I shrugged. "I guess he just decided he wasn't meant to have a dog."

CHAPTER TWENTY-TWO

So it was up to me, and me alone, to do something about Sam the dogman and the dogfighting gang with only a few days left to go. Since I'd decided not to let Phoebe find out that there was such terrifying evil in the world, and most definitely couldn't tell Edwin or my mother, I'd have to figure out what to do all on my own.

Of course, I knew that even a tough eleven-year-old girl like me couldn't take down a gang of criminals completely alone, and I wasn't kidding myself. There was no doubt in my mind that I was going to need help and plenty of it. This was epic, no joke, and I'd needed to think seriously about what to do.

The Costa boys had gone off island to their family reunion in Rhode Island and most of my other friends from school wouldn't be back from trips with their parents until Derby time. I'd heard that Owen Munroe and his dad had returned from their fishing trip, but Owen was a wimp who was scared of his own shadow. Coraline Reed was helping her mother with the family gardening business 24/7, and Jos Phillips was allergic to bees so had to be watched carefully during the summer months. She'd swell up like a beach ball if stung and turn all kinds of disgusting colors. Most of the other kids hanging around couldn't be trusted to keep a secret, no less help me with such an important operation.

My only option was Sheriff Ernestine Cobbs, the very one who had arrested Willis. Not exactly my favorite person in the world.

So I wasn't eager to ask the sheriff for help but figured that I didn't have a choice.

Sam the dogman would be waiting at the ferry dock on Tuesday night, and there'd be no telling what the dogman would do to me if I didn't show up or came without the promised Honey.

While Sam didn't have my address or even my real name, I'd given him our landline phone number and he could definitely track me down if he wanted to.

I left Phoebe, Honey, and the kittens and headed down the long hill from the bluff into town.

The walk to the jail was about two miles, but I'd decided against hopping the bus again since my last trip had taken forever. Despite the dust and dirt flying up to my face, the banks on either side of the road were overgrown and crammed with all kinds of different colors. I loved it when all the island wildflowers exploded: pink, white, yellow, red, blue, even purple if you looked in the right places. All so different, but together they looked like each one belonged.

I wasn't exactly nervous about talking to the sheriff, more determined than anything, and I guess maybe a little worried too. It was still very possible that I could get into a heap of trouble since I'd tried to sell Honey without permission, but that just didn't seem very important when I thought about the dogmen and the dogs that needed help. Just remembering what I'd read at the library made me mad all over again, and I broke into a run, passing Coastal Convenience and rounding the bend toward the harbor and the center of town.

PART FOUR

SHEPHERDS

CHAPTER TWENTY-THREE

Sheriff Cobbs wasn't exactly happy to see me.

I'd forgotten that it was Saturday and the front office of the jail was completely empty except for the small woman sitting at her large desk.

"No, Bean, you cannot see your brother without an approved adult. I already told your mother that when he was first arrested—if you want to see Willis, she will need to come with you. That's the rule."

She was peering up from behind her big desk, and when I say peering up, I meant exactly that. It seemed to me that the Hancock County's office should have bought her a taller chair because looked like she was sinking way down, only the top of her little, pointed head visible.

"Sheriff Cobbs," I announced in my most official manner, "I'm not here to visit Willis. I came to talk to you about something else."

She turned to shuffle a pile of papers. "Nope," she said without looking up. "I'm sorry, Bean Wright, but you can't lobby for him to be released either. Willis committed a crime and must face the consequences. Now skedaddle, young lady. I've got a ton of work to get done before evening."

Nothing peeved me more than being called *young lady*. Well, nothing except being called young man.

"Sheriff Cobbs." I cleared my throat and tried to lean across the desk. "Please. I've come to report a crime."

And so the sheriff sat back in her chair and listened. She listened to me as if I wasn't just a kid, but someone important with something important to say. She even took notes on a long yellow pad as I talked, which I found to be pretty flattering. There were a few times when her desk phone rang, and she just ignored it and motioned to me to keep on talking.

When I'd finished, Sheriff Cobbs pulled out a stool and asked me to sit down directly next to her so that we were eye to eye. I hadn't even realized that I'd been standing the whole time and suddenly felt exhausted.

"Bean," she said slowly, looking hard into my face, "these are very serious accusations, and I don't take them lightly. Are you sure that you have all your facts straight?" Her voice was surprisingly low, just above a whisper, and it had a sugary sweet tone, maybe a tad condescending, but I was trying my best to overlook that.

I nodded. "I'm sure."

"Do you have any solid evidence? Anything concrete to back up what you just told me? If what you're reporting is all true, then we need some hard evidence before proceeding. To tell you the truth, your story sounds a little inconsistent in places and there's really nothing the police can do, anyway, without getting more facts about this so-called dogman and his plan to purchase your dog."

"Well, the dog isn't exactly mine." I may have omitted that detail.

"Whose dog is it?" The sheriff looked confused.

"My friend's, but she agreed that we should . . ."

"Have you spoken to your mother about any of this?"

"No, but . . ."

"Bean." Sheriff Cobbs leaned over, took my hand in hers, and squeezed. Her hands were tiny and cold, a miniature vise. She looked different up close, kinda old and kinda tired. Her small face was pale and chalky, and her dark eyes were large, smudged with thick black eyeliner. But most disturbing was that her skin was caked with this powdery stuff that she'd really piled on, an especially big mess of it towering over an ugly zit, right in the middle of her forehead. And at first glance, her small mouth didn't seem to have lips since they were sucked right up inside each time she spoke, each word making a wet smack. The sheriff smelled a little like calamine lotion, the junk you put on sunburn or bug bites. Not a bad smell, not a good one either, just perfume masked with something else.

"Bean, I know this must be a tough time for you with Willis's arrest. But you can get into real serious trouble by making up or even exaggerating stories, particularly when it comes to the law and the police. If what you tell me is really true, however, I'll do my best to help, but I'm afraid my hands are completely tied without some evidence. I'll start looking into possible dogfighting activities in the general area when I have time— Why don't you just go home now, help your mother around the house and have some fun going to the beach with your friends. I'll let you know if I come up with anything significant." She dropped my hands and turned back to the pile of papers threatening to fall in her lap. "Understand?"

I understood all right. She didn't have to spell it out for me. I understood that I was on my own and would have to rescue the sick and hurting animals all by myself. Have some fun on the beach? Ha.

It seemed my only option for any help at all was to talk to Phoebe, the very person who I'd thought couldn't handle such upsetting news.

The thing about Phoebe was that she was a lot smarter than she looked. I knew that from almost the first week I met her. And that was a good thing, since she often looked pretty dumb.

So the very next morning, I took a deep breath and told Phoebe everything, After I finally finished spilling all the gory details about Sam, the keep, springboards, treadmills, conventions, champions, dogmen, dogfight rings, and gangs, I was prepared for the worst. Would she cry hysterically or rant and rave? Would she throw something at me and toss me out of Beach Bluff right on my rump, never to talk to me again? I had no idea.

And yet, surprisingly, after I spat it all out, Phoebe didn't say or do anything for a few minutes. She just went completely still and so quiet that I immediately regretted my decision to fill her in. Maybe it was just selfish of me to reveal it all in its gruesome detail. After all, she was only nine.

But once I'd started talking, I couldn't seem to stop. I just went on and on, even letting it slip that I'd needed the Honey sale money to get Willis out of jail, something I hadn't shared with another single living soul. And then I tried to explain why I'd changed my mind, going to the police out of desperation after reading about dogfighting gangs online. I'd told her all about Sheriff Cobbs and how I tried to get her to help. By the time I was finished, I realized that my whole body, from head to toe, was shaking. The lump in my throat was so big that no matter how hard I tried to swallow, it wouldn't budge.

Finally, Phoebe looked down at her hands, then back up at me. I was startled to see how white her face had become; even her freckles seemed to disappear. Her gray eyes had narrowed, and her mouth was set in a firm, tight line.

"Phoebe," I almost whispered, frightened of what she might have to say, "I'm so sorry. I'm sorry that I lied to you, and I'm really sorry that I even thought about selling Honey. It's all my fault. And now I just don't know what to do. What should we do? It's already Sunday!"

We had been sitting, as usual, on the kitchen floor, and I watched as Phoebe uncrossed her legs and slowly rose. Without a single word, she walked over to Honey, who was snoring happily, two kittens snuggled on top of her head and one lying across her snout like an upside-down smile. Phoebe bent down to kiss the big dog on one closed eye and then the other, her mother's long silver skirt trailing behind like a bridal train, then turned to walk back to me. Instinctively, I stiffened, perhaps expecting a slap or kick of some kind, although that was entirely out of her nature. She looked at me for a moment, probably seeing a pathetic crumple of a girl rather than her strong, confident, eleven-year-old friend, and reached down for both of my hands, pulling me up so that we were both standing face-to-face.

I braced myself.

"The only thing I care about," Phoebe said, so calmly and quietly that I had trouble hearing her, "is that we rescue all of Sam's dogs and puppies. You tried to help your brother, Beanie, and maybe you still will, but for now we have to help the animals. You and I are going to make sure that all the dogs are safe. Promise me that."

And then Phoebe D. Sinclair wrapped her skinny arms around me so tightly that it was difficult to breathe, her mess of curls mashing into my neck. I stood perfectly still. She was probably a foot shorter than me and weighed about ten pounds less, but at that one moment, my friend seemed taller and stronger than most folks I'd ever known.

I had carefully planned my confession to Phoebe at the same time as the Rock Haven's farmer's market, since I knew Edwin would be out of earshot. There was no doubt in my mind that he'd find all the market's "locally resourced goods" irresistible, as he did every week, and remain away from Beach Bluff for at least thirty minutes. When he returned, two large recyclable shopping bags filled to the brim, he immediately called out, "What's shaking, *mates*?" Then he began unloading the groceries on the kitchen counter. "Staying out of trouble?"

We must have nodded too quickly, because he stopped for a second midstream and stared at us suspiciously. Phoebe and I were sitting at the kitchen table, whispering about Sam's date with me on the ferry dock and trying to concoct a dog rescue plan by drawing a diagram, although I wasn't exactly sure how a diagram was going to help with anything. Phoebe, on the other hand, told me that her tutor from home had shown her how to map out her homework ideas by drawing big bubbles with connecting lines. The results looked like a mess of complicated nothing to me.

"Ever go on a revenge mission, Edwin?" Phoebe suddenly asked, as calm as can be.

"What? What are you talking about, young lady?" Edwin was clearly perplexed. I shot Phoebe an alarmed look.

"Got a Taser, Edwin?" Phoebe asked then, without even looking up.

"A Taser?" Edwin and I spoke at the same time, with the same tone of alarm.

"JK." Phoebe laughed, continuing to look down at her diagram. "Sheesh. I was just kidding."

"You're certainly full of surprises, Phoebe." Edwin sighed, concentrating on a huge stalk of celery. "You scared me for a minute."

I sighed with relief, frightened that our cover was about to be blown.

"What about a bow and arrow? Brass knuckles?"

Enough was enough. Phoebe was clearly losing her mind. I kicked her under the table and made the cut-it-out sign by swiping my index finger across my neck. Honey raised her head and waddled over to where I was sitting, I slid my chair around to greet the big dog, and a velvety fold of fur brushed my hand. She sniffed it for a second, turning back to check for the kittens, then spread one warm, doughy jowl over my arm so that I was immediately drenched.

"Thanks a lot." I laughed, reaching to scratch the top of her head. The kittens, having spied their fearless leader, slid out of their box and pranced happily over to us in a crooked little dance. Honey edged her cheek off me, leaving a damp stain on my sleeve, but then she suddenly turned back again, her black fist of a nose quivering. And before you could say *Neapolitan mastiff*, she let out the deepest howl imaginable, so sorrowful that my arms prickled with goose bumps. It seemed as if her bellow could have shaken the entire house, widow's walk and all.

"What's wrong, Honey?" I asked her shakily, taken aback by the howl, something I had never heard before. Maybe she was sick or had stepped on something sharp when outside. Or maybe it was even possible that she sensed I'd been betraying her by talking with Sam the dogman and that she could be in danger. But when I felt a faint tug on my pants cuff, I immediately understood.

The smallest of Honey's kittens, the one I liked the most with the three black paws and one white, had broken away from her tiny posse and was climbing up my leg, hanging on in a dangerous position by one single claw. The other two were curled around Honey's back leg, mewing like nobody's business. "It's okay," I whispered, reaching down to cup the stray kitten in my hands. "Don't worry, Honey, I know that this baby belongs to you." And I bent to place the kitten by the other two, where they welcomed her with a flutter of little paws.

Honey raised her head slowly to look at me and then to my surprise, heaved up the entire front half her massive body into a kind of awkward animal hug so that only her bottom legs were left on the floor and her wide front paws balanced on my shoulders, a crumpled, humongous mug pressing into my face so it was hard to breathe. A waterfall of drool rushed down and over my chin and I inhaled Honey's unmistakable animal scent: musk, brine, island moss after a rain. Thankfully, she shifted her muzzle to one side but continued to stand there, her body spread over my own and my entire torso covered with silver fur. It might have been hard for someone just coming into the room to tell where each of us started and the other left off, who was human and who was not.

CHAPTER TWENTY-FOUR

That night, I tossed and turned, Willis, Honey, Sam, court, sentencing . . . everyone, all of it, on my mind. I'd hatched a brilliant plan to rescue my brother, and now I needed another to save all the dogs from dogfighting. Time was getting short and I still hadn't figured out exactly how to save Willis without sacrificing Honey. In fact, I still hadn't figured out exactly what I was going to do about anything.

"Have you ever been sentenced by a judge?" I asked my mother early the next morning, before heading out to the bluff. She was sitting at the old square table, studying the *Register* in her tan bathrobe. My mother looked up quickly, her cheeks pink, as if she'd just been caught doing something she shouldn't. She caught me staring and grinned, revealing a crooked front tooth, the one that was tinged gray and that always reminded me of Willis, who had the exact same impish smile and same tooth that overlapped over the next as if trying to crawl away.

"No, I've never been sentenced, Bean, and I've never been arrested. Kind of a strange question to be asking your mother, don't you think?"

"Guess so. Just wondering."

"Well, stop wondering and pour me another cup of coffee,

will you? Got to get to work in a few minutes and need a double shot of caffeine for the day."

Once, when no one was looking, I took a gulp of coffee, and believe me, I'll never do that again. It tasted more like medicine than anything I'd want morning after morning as my mother did. But I had to admit, it smelled sort of nice as I poured her a fresh cup from the old coffeepot bubbling on the counter. "But you've been in court before, right? I know you went for the other Willis stuff."

"Yes," she said, reaching eagerly for the mug. "Yes, unfortunately for the other Willis stuff."

"So, what does it mean to have real evidence in court?"

"What are you up to, Bean? Why are you asking about evidence, of all things?"

"Dunno. Just curious."

"Well, if you're thinking about getting Willis out of jail by trying to mess around with the court system, just forget about it. Your brother made a serious mistake and now has to pay the consequences."

Although I hadn't exactly been thinking about Willis right then, my heart dropped at the mention of his name and of his "paying the consequences." I could tell that my mother saw my face fall, because she continued quickly,

"But, I promise you, all this will seem like a bad dream, and it won't be too long before Willis will be back home again right there in his bed next you, just like always. We'll be back to normal as if none of this ever happened. One day before too long."

I thought about that for a minute. I knew that my mother was trying to make me feel better, but somehow didn't think what she was saying could be true. It was hard to imagine Willis coming home and sharing our room again like nothing had ever happened. Something *had* happened and not just to him.

"But how does someone, you know, how does someone ever really prove anything? How does the judge get convinced since no one really knows what truly happened or the real truth? What kind of evidence to prove someone did wrong?"

"I'm not exactly sure, Bean, but know that hard facts are needed. Anyone can say anything for his or her own benefit, but evidence is objective information, like a photograph, fingerprints, DNA, or an eyewitness report. The legal system's pretty confusing, and it's not a given that the truth will ever come out in many cases. Sad to say, but the bad guys sometimes get away with fudging the truth, especially when they can afford the best lawyers and advocates that money can buy. And those who don't have money or anyone to help fight their cause, well, I'm sorry to say that they are the ones often left by the wayside. But that's not the situation with Willis. He broke the law and is guilty. No two ways about it."

I knew what a lawyer did for criminals but wasn't absolutely sure what the word *advocate* meant. I was just about to ask when I heard a loud knock followed by another. My mother and I looked at each other in surprise, then turned to see Sheriff Cobbs's slight shadow behind the screen door.

Didn't the woman have somewhere else to be without bugging us at home? It was still pretty early in the morning, after all. I knew that the sheriff and my mother were friends, but did that have to mean her never leaving us alone in the privacy of our own house?

So there I was, face-to-face with our pint-sized sheriff all over again, and believe me, I was not happy with the surprise. I figured that in just a few minutes, my cover would be blown and my mother would know everything about Honey, Sam, and dogfighting. The sheriff and I eyed each other across the kitchen while my mother poured her a cup of coffee. I guessed she found the bitter drink as irresistible as every other grown-up I knew.

"Everything okay, Bean?" the sheriff asked me, slowly bringing the mug to her lips as she sat down at the table.

My mother looked over at me suspiciously. Unfortunately, she was the type who never missed a trick. My heart dropped.

"Everything's okay," I replied quickly, desperately hoping that guilt wasn't popping up all over my face in hives. "But I think I'd better go to my room for a while since I have to make my bed and do a bunch of important things." Ha. My mother would definitely see through that. I hadn't made my bed in weeks. But before anyone could say anything, I scooted out of the kitchen as fast as possible and then hid right behind my bedroom door, out of sight, but still listening to what was being said.

Luckily, and to my huge relief, it turned out that the sheriff hadn't come to our house that morning to mention anything at all about my recent visit to her office or about Sam and dog-fighting. She'd come to talk to my mother about Willis and what would happen at his sentencing.

I heard the sheriff say that she'd finally gotten a court date for Willis and that his sentencing would be in another month. Although she wasn't sure, it didn't look as though there would be any chance my brother would get off scot-free, although we'd all hoped that his jail time before sentencing would be enough "time served." Instead, there'd probably be two options for Willis at sentencing, one that he'd have to do community service, and the other being his going to a special school in Maine where he could finish his last year of high school and graduate.

"You mean juvie?!" I popped right out of my room across the narrow hallway into the kitchen again. There was no way my brother was going to juvenile detention, especially to Maine, all the way in America.

"Bean!" My mother was clearly unhappy with my eaves-dropping. "This is an adult conversation, and we really don't need your two cents right now."

But the sheriff just nodded and said that she understood that juvenile detention away from home sounded scary, but that she knew of a very special, small, alternative school that was designed for gifted students who had a great deal of poten-tial but who had made some serious mistakes in their lives. She told us that the place offered counseling as part of the curricu-lum, so any issues troubling Willis could be addressed. And since he was starting his senior year of high school in September, he could complete it there, in nine months. Then he would graduate and be free to come home or do anything he wanted.

"Why does he have to go that far away?"

"The school really isn't that far, Bean, all things considered," the sheriff said. "And I'm sure arrangements could be made for you and your mother to visit him from time to time."

"What about the *Pirate Flag*?" I blurted out, my stomach churning and my chest beginning to itch. Willis had just been elected as the editor of *Pirate Flag*, the high school literary magazine. "And Senior Day and the senior prom?"

I knew that Willis was looking forward to all those things and his last year of high school.

"Well, he could stay home in Rock Haven," the sheriff said, shaking her head, making it obvious that she didn't like the idea. "But he wouldn't be allowed back at Haven High until he completed his community service requirements—that would take him at least six to nine months. So he wouldn't be able to return to school until the following year."

Practically everyone in Rock Haven knew that Willis was a terrific student and planned to attend Harvard University after graduation, if he could finagle a scholarship. He'd been talking about college since he was a little kid.

I looked at my mother anxiously. She had wrapped her bathrobe across her chest, holding the collar tightly up to her neck with both hands, as though protecting herself from the cold. "What kind of community service?"

"Mostly janitorial in the courthouse, mopping and the like. Also picking up trash in the roads and assisting with maintenance and septic issues at the jail. And other assorted tasks as needed."

Sheriff Cobbs scrunched her nose like she was smelling something foul, which made sense since anything septic-related stunk. I couldn't really imagine Willis spending a whole year mopping, picking up trash, and dealing with the jail's disgusting septic issues. Yuck. Double yuck. But my brother being away in another state for his last year of high school also seemed unimaginable.

"Would he be on probation and have a curfew? I mean, if he stayed on island?" My mother's voice quivered, and I could see that the color of her eyes was switching from green to brown.

"Yes." Sheriff Cobbs was trying to look all official, sitting up straight and blinking quickly. "He wouldn't be able to go anywhere but home, Nell. Sorry to say that it would be straight from home to community service and back home again every day for the whole time. I understand that you'd hoped for a different result and we all know that Willis is a good boy with a great future, and I'd hate to see him confined and limited like that. But it's up to you." The sheriff looked at my mother and then at me. "It's up to you and, of course, Willis as well." She wiped a few beads of sweat off her forehead with the back of her hand, leaving a horizontal streak. "Just let me know what you think and if there's anything I can do to help."

For a minute, and I mean just for one short minute, I felt

like giving Sheriff Cobbs what for. It didn't seem fair that Willis couldn't continue a normal life—after all, he'd already been in jail for almost a month. But then she reached over for her hat, placed it evenly on her ridiculously tiny head, squared her spindly shoulders, and nodded.

"Let me know what you think is best," she said, turning toward the door. "You still have a month before sentencing, so give the matter some serious thought."

"Wait," my mother said, standing up so suddenly that I jumped. "I don't have to think about it at all, Ernestine. Willis will go away to school and graduate in time for college."

The sheriff nodded again. For a minute, silence stretched out its long hands, then closed around my own neck. I wanted to speak. I wanted to object. How in the world was it okay with my mother to send Willis to some special school far away from his family? But all I could do was stand there.

"There goes a real good sheriff," my mother said softly after the door closed. "She's got a lot on her plate but still took the time to stop by and talk to us in person. She's tough, but she's got a big heart."

I didn't reply but disagreed 200 percent. Sheriff Cobbs didn't seem all that tough or bighearted to me, and the options she gave us for Willis were terrible. I didn't know if my mother had made the right choice or not since it seemed that both choices stunk.

I must have been frowning because my mother reached over to brush the bangs off my forehead. "You know, Bean," she said, "it isn't the sheriff's fault that Willis is in this situation. And the sentencing consequences may be for the best, no matter how difficult. It's the only way he'll learn to respect the law."

"Whatever." I could hardly breathe, thinking about Willis rotting in jail for another whole month and then being sent away off island. I absolutely needed to get him home pronto so we could brainstorm together about how to get around the sentencing. Willis could always figure out stuff, and I was pretty sure he'd come up with a plan to avoid going to school in Maine. I just needed to get him out of jail and home quickly.

But how was I going to do this, considering the new information I had about dogfighting? Bail money or not, there was no way I could sell Honey to Sam. Just the idea of her being used for dogfighting made me want to hurl.

CHAPTER TWENTY-FIVE

It was only a day before Sam was to turn up on the ferry dock to buy Honey, and Phoebe and I were desperately trying to figure out how to collect evidence that would nab the dogman.

Not to speak of how I'd get the money for bail without going through with Honey's sale.

In the middle of the night before, I'd bolted upright in bed, thinking I'd seen Willis standing over me, wearing his Harvard banner around his shoulders like a shawl. Of course, it had been just a stupid dream, but my heart was pounding furiously, and I started to bawl, never having had felt so alone as I did at that moment. How could I leave my brother in jail another day? If I didn't rescue him, who would? And what would I actually do when face-to-face with Sam?

But maybe, just maybe, I could get all the evidence needed to eventually put Sam away, as Phoebe and I had planned, and still get to keep the money. The only thing I could come up with was to go through with Honey's sale, then pocket Sam's cash and run off before the big girl could be snatched. After it was all said and done, I'd hand over some kind of proof to the sheriff so that Sam would be arrested later. I knew that it would be dangerous and all three of us, Phoebe, Honey, and me, would be at risk, but at least I could try. I had to try.

The only problem was how in the world to manage all this. Pretending to be someone you aren't isn't easy, and I didn't exactly look like a hardened criminal. Would Sam bolt when he saw a kid instead of an adult? And how in the world could I collect hard evidence to put Sam away?

Phoebe and I were sitting on Beach Bluff's front porch for privacy since Edwin was inside, banging around the kitchen and whipping up an "original creation." Fiercely chewing on her fingernails like there was no tomorrow and tapping her feet on the old porch floorboards, Phoebe mumbled to herself like an old woman. I couldn't understand a single word.

"Are you okay?" I asked her. I hadn't been feeling very okay myself. My stomach was racing in jumbled circles.

"No. I'm not." She stopped tapping for a second and stared straight ahead at nothing but Beach Bluff's overgrown front walkway with a vacant look on her face. "It's just that it makes me so furious. So angry that someone would hurt animals like that, just for money! I was working on my diagram last night, and then I started thinking about those poor dogs and those awful dogfighting men and just began to get angrier and angrier." She glanced up at me pitifully. "I know I shouldn't have said anything to Edwin yesterday. That wasn't very smart. But I couldn't help it. I can't help wanting to go after those bad guys, without caring about anything else."

"We just have to keep brainstorming," I told her quietly.

"I just don't understand why the sheriff couldn't do something right away. You've already told her everything. Isn't it her job to get evidence? How are we supposed to come up with anything that she'd believe, anyway?"

I shrugged. I didn't want to admit that I had no idea.

"Maybe we could set up a stakeout." Phoebe's voice was suddenly stronger, almost hopeful. "You know, the way they do in the movies and TV. We could follow the creep and catch him in the act. Don't you watch *Law & Order*?"

My mother was pretty strict about what I watched on the old television set with the cracked screen that she kept in her bedroom, and I was almost embarrassed to tell Phoebe that *Law & Order* wasn't on the list. It irked me that a nine-year-old was allowed to see such an adult program when I wasn't.

"Frances, you know, the Irish nanny before Elsa, well, she didn't really care what I watched on TV. I remember one *Law & Order* show where this guy with tattoos went on a stakeout so he could catch the bad woman who stole a bunch of money and did some other things too. And it worked, it really worked. I don't remember how but the woman was caught and sent to prison. What'd you think, Beanie? Maybe a stakeout."

Unfortunately, I didn't think that a stakeout was a very practical solution. First of all, it would probably mean getting the sheriff involved, and second, Sam apparently lived far away somewhere in America. But I didn't want to discourage Phoebe, and at least she'd come up with something. I hadn't even been able to do that.

"Not a bad thought," I told her, trying to sound hopeful. "But I'm not sure that the sheriff would agree to help, and we'd probably have to get her on board. She wouldn't even help find Sam without more information and evidence, let alone agree to a stakeout. Not very likely that she'd go for the idea. Maybe we should try to think of something else."

We were both quiet for a minute, and just as Phoebe raised a second row of barely-there fingernails to her mouth, I had a thought. When I'd asked my mother about what kind of evidence would be needed in court, she mentioned DNA.

"Hey," I said. "Why don't we pretend to go through with Honey's sale, and then get Sam captured after with DNA evidence? We could pull out a strand of his hair and give it to the sheriff." I may have not watched Phoebe's favorite crime TV shows, but talking with my mother reminded me that I'd learned all about DNA from Willis, who'd studied it in science. "Do you know what DNA is?"

Phoebe rolled her eyes. I guess she knew.

"Well, so what do you think? Good plan or not?" I was pretty sure that I'd hit the nail on the head, and it was a good idea.

Phoebe just shook her head slowly and tucked a stray ringlet behind her ear. "Don't think so," she said. "That sounds kind of gross. I'm not sure we want to mess with some creep's actual greasy hair."

The kid had a point. "I guess you're right," I finally agreed. Just the thought of my hands on Sam's scalp made me feel queasy. I'd just have to think of something else.

So we sat there for a while, Phoebe tapping her feet and biting her fingernails and me getting more and more nervous. If we didn't figure out something soon, Sam would get away with his terrible crimes. Not to mention Willis being left in jail.

It was Phoebe who finally came up with the idea that made the most sense. "I'll come with you to the docks when you meet him!" she announced out of the blue, leaping out of her chair and standing right in front of me. "You see, I'll be your second in command."

I wasn't so sure. It was going to be difficult enough luring Honey from Beach Bluff and getting her all the way to the dock, then safely back home again; the thought of adding Phoebe to the mix made me nervous. She wasn't exactly cool and collected when it came to Honey, or anything else for that matter. And Phoebe had no idea that I was thinking of keeping the cash for Willis.

I hadn't slept much the night before and could feel my nerves beginning to prickle. The last thing I needed was a nine-year-old trying to weasel her way into the action and complicate everything. Things were complicated enough as they were.

"Umm," I said slowly, looking the other way, "I'm not sure it's such a good idea for you to come."

"Why not?"

Arguing with Phoebe wasn't going to end well. I'd learned these past few weeks that convincing her of anything wasn't exactly a piece of cake, and I'd have to figure out some good excuse to get her off my back or there'd be no end to her pestering. "There's no point to your coming along, Phoebe. Better for you to stick it out at Beach Bluff in case Edwin gets wind that something's not right. I need my second in command to stay back at the house."

Phoebe thought about this for a minute and then started hopping up and down, something she did when excited. Her blouse sleeves, wide and edged with white lace, flapped wildly, reminding me of one of the giant seagulls that flew over Refuge Beach.

"Well, how are you going to get evidence for the sheriff without me?" She practically chortled. "You know, I have my own cell phone, although it's only for emergencies. Edwin keeps it in the kitchen butler's pantry with the good china."

Suddenly, I caught Phoebe's drift. Why hadn't I thought of this myself? "We can record him," I said quickly. "I get it. We can get Sam to tell me everything while you video him with your phone. That would be a kind of evidence."

Phoebe had actually come up with a pretty good idea, but I wasn't really exactly sure how it would work. She was only a kid and hardly able to dress herself correctly, no less gather criminal evidence. But I also knew that when Phoebe put her mind to something, she usually pulled it off. Maybe better to have her tag along with me than to leave her at home with Edwin, anyway. If the trip to the dock and back took me too long, she might get nervous and end up letting the cat out of the bag.

Phoebe nodded enthusiastically. "Yes," she said. "I've seen all kinds of people do that on *Law & Order* by hiding a video recorder somewhere when the bad guy confesses. One of us can get him to talk about his dogfighting gang and the other can be somewhere near, hiding out and videoing everything with the phone." She stopped hopping for a minute and started to nibble at her fingernails. "But we have to figure all this out right now, how we're both going to sneak out of our houses without anyone noticing and how we're going to lug Honey all the way to the dock and back home again." Phoebe crossed her arms around her chest and sighed. "I hate to be mean," she continued softly, "but Honey can be a real pain when you want her to get moving. We better plan on an hour or so just to get from Beach Bluff to the ferry."

I couldn't help smiling. The trip from the old house to the docks was no more than a ten-minute walk. Honey was most certainly not much of an athlete, but a full hour seemed like overkill. As it turned out, Phoebe was pretty much correct, as she most usually was. Irritating, but true.

The morning of Sam's arrival, I called my mother at Stop & Shop, something that annoyed her to no end, since phoning her at work was a big no-no. But I hadn't wanted to lie to her face-to-face at home; my mother always said that she always knew if I was telling the truth by just looking into my eyes.

When I reached her at Stop & Shop, at first she was kind of alarmed, then just plain old irritated.

"I'm glad you're okay and that you let me know that you're

sleeping over at your friend's, Bean, but I'm in the middle of dealing with a return right now. How someone can expect to exchange a cabbage for a bag of carrots, I'll never know, but it is what it is. Have a good night and I'll catch up with you tomorrow."

Edwin didn't seem to care when Phoebe and I told him about the sleepover, although he made sure that I'd checked with my mother.

"Any requests for dinner?" he asked. "Catfish or burgers with catsup for your mewsment?"

Phoebe and I just rolled our eyes. Honey's kittens had become new material for Edwin to tease us, and we were already used to it.

The rest of the day was a blur. Phoebe and I stayed in her room for most of it, only checking on the kittens downstairs now and then. I sat hunched on her bed, trying to concentrate on each step of our plan for the evening and exactly how we were going to pull it off. And I tried not to think about my brother, at least not for a while.

Our plan was clear: Phoebe and I would bring Honey down to the ferry dock, where I'd meet up with Sam and somehow get him admit to his dogfighting crimes, while pretending to be Spike, the dogman's assistant. Not exactly a breeze, but I thought I could pull it off. Phoebe would hide nearby and record the whole thing on her cell phone. Then I'd tempt Honey with a giant-sized raspberry Fiber One bar, her very favorite kind, and run home with Phoebe, Honey right behind. On a few occasions, I'd witnessed the big dog perk up and move pretty fast if anything raspberry was in close sight.

It was a risky business. I knew that. What if Sam got really angry? What if Honey refused to move or was too slow and Sam ended up catching all of us? And what about my brother? How would I rescue him after all? Could I bring myself to pocket Sam's tainted cash? If I did, it would be stealing since there was no way I'd hand over Honey to Sam or any other dogman. And even worse, I'd be taking money from someone who probably made it from dogfighting.

That night, Phoebe and I paced nervously together in her room, waiting to leave until it was 9:30 p.m., when we'd planned to sneak out of the house. We didn't say much of anything to each other, both of us checking the small alarm clock on her bedside table every few minutes and then pacing all over again.

But even as I'd wanted to save Honey and all the other dogs from dogfighting, I couldn't help picturing Willis alone in his cell. I started to think about my decision all over again. Was I doing the right thing? If Phoebe and I went ahead with our plans to rescue all the dogs, I wouldn't be able to rescue my brother, unless I kept Sam's rotten money. No getting around that.

I imagined Willis hunched on a concrete bench, hanging his head and tapping his feet on the floor, the way he did whenever he was impatient or mad. My heart dropped and a sour taste filled my mouth. How could I abandon my very own flesh and blood, letting him rot in jail instead of doing everything I possibly could to get him out? Were dogs and dogfighting really that important? After all, they were animals, and my brother was human. My very favorite human. But next, my mind's eye saw Willis stand up, hands on his hips, his eyes clear as seawater. He raised his head and flung back his shoulders. "Be true to yourself, Bean. Be the person you want to be, no matter what anyone else says or tells you. I'm proud of my little sis. You're strong and you're smart. Hang in and follow what you know is right."

But right and wrong weren't always clear. If I stole Sam's fifteen hundred dollars, I'd be on the wrong side of the law and also probably pocketing cash made from harming dogs. I wished with all my might that I could talk to my brother, just for a second, to ask his advice. But I knew that there was no time left and I'd have to make my decision about keeping the money all on my own. My stomach tightened and my heart pounded, but my head was clear and, strangely enough, I didn't feel or see a single hive anywhere, double-checking my arms and legs. I stood up quickly to make sure I wasn't dizzy. Nope. Not the least bit dizzy or nauseous. No sign of vertigo.

Phoebe was biting her nails like there was no tomorrow, sitting cross-legged on her bed. I took a deep breath and sat down again next to her.

"It's going to be okay, right?" she asked me in a small voice. I couldn't see her face in the dim light and dropped my arm over her shoulders—a puzzle of birdlike bones underneath.

"It's going to be okay," I told her firmly, although I wasn't so sure. "Just stick by me and everything will be fine."

And so, we sat together in the darkening room until it was finally time to go. Phoebe took the twenty-dollar bill that had been in Mr. Spencer's envelope out of one of her Altoids boxes, surprising me with how neatly it was folded, reminding me of the Japanese origami crane we'd made during International Week at school. She'd pleated her money into the shape of a crane, and I remembered that it represented good fortune.

If only.

We had discussed bringing along the forty dollars in case of emergency. After all, what if we had to make a quick getaway and jump in a taxi or bribe someone for something, although I wasn't really sure for what. Knowing that we had Mr. Spencer's forty big ones with us was comforting, a kind of backup if there was trouble. And who knew what Sam would do or say once I met with him. Maybe our entire plan would fall apart, and we'd just have to beat it out of sight without the sheriff's evidence.

Or maybe, just maybe, I'd take the thousand dollars for Willis and save five hundred to give to Phoebe later without confessing how I got it.

My twenty-dollar bill was crumpled, and when I pulled it out of my jeans pocket, it fell to the floor in a tiny green heap.

Phoebe picked the bill up quickly, smoothed it with her hand, and folded it neatly just like she had done with her own. Then she slipped everything into the side pocket of her shorts.

"Hey, Beanie," Phoebe said softly, almost in a whisper, "you know it was Mr. Spencer who rescued Honey."

"Huh?" I had no idea what she was talking about. "What? *When* did *who* rescue Honey?"

"Mr. Spencer. You know, the day we found the kittens and it was raining real hard someone brought Honey onto the porch so she'd keep dry. When she tore off the porch thingie and came inside the kitchen."

I frowned and looked at Phoebe. "Mr. Spencer? How do you know? I thought Edwin had brought her up there." Phoebe shook her head quickly.

"Nope. Couldn't have been Edwin. I've been thinking about it. Remember, Edwin was busy helping me save the kittens from inside the wall that morning. See, Edwin and I were rescuing the kittens, Mr. Spencer was rescuing Honey, and Honey, well, I think that Honey is kinda rescuing us."

"What are you talking about, Phoebe?" I was getting annoyed. We didn't have time to chat about some silly rescuing story.

"Every evening after you went home," Phoebe continued, ignoring my impatient sigh, "Mr. Spencer used to come over to give Honey a treat, usually a piece of toast or a dog cookie. Before his accident, that is. I guess he saw that Honey had to stay outside on the front walkway all day so that she could guard us and thought she needed a reward. And he always bent over to pet her and whisper something in her ear. Maybe he just told her what a great dog she is or how much he likes her. Dunno. But I bet it was him, I bet it was Mr. Spencer who led Honey up the porch that day of the storm. It must have been pretty hard for him, since his ankle was so hurt. He must be a pretty brave man to care about an animal so much."

I thought about that for a minute and then shrugged. Maybe Phoebe was right and maybe she wasn't. For now, I really didn't care.

It was exactly 9:29 p.m. when we slunk out of Beach Bluff to meet the arrival of the 10:30 p.m. ferry from America, shakily holding our shoes in our hands so as to be as quiet as possible. Phoebe had told me that Edwin was always in his room by 8:30 p.m. every night, listening to some kind of opera music and taking a "delightful, tepid" bath. She knew about the bath because he'd told her so, pouring himself a cup of tea before heading upstairs at the same time each evening. She said that *La Bohème* was Edwin's favorite, as if I'd know the name of one opera from another, and that the story was "very, very tragic." I figured that made sense, since Edwin could be pretty dramatic himself.

As we passed Edwin's bedroom in the dark hallway, I sighed with relief that his door was closed and heard some poor woman singing in the saddest voice possible. Glancing over at Phoebe in a moment of alarm, she just shrugged and mouthed, "*La Bohème.*" The voice wafted through the doorway, giving us even more cover in case the old wood floors squeaked as we passed.

We managed to get down the staircase without a problem and scurried quietly to the kitchen, where Honey was sleeping with her kittens on the floor. I knew that getting Honey away from her brood wasn't going to be easy, and for a second, I once again reconsidered my plan. What if something went wrong and Sam grabbed her leash without forking over the cash? What if he had a weapon? I took a deep breath and tried to calm down.

As planned, Phoebe gathered up the kittens and snuggled them into their "nursery room" one by one, and when Honey raised her head an inch or so off the floor to supervise, I snapped her leash onto her collar, noticing that Edwin had exchanged the old, worn leather one for a hot-pink, rhinestoned item that looked more like a necklace than a dog collar.

I had worried that the big dog would be upset to be away from the kittens for the night, but Phoebe, being Phoebe, had researched this ahead of time and found that mother dogs are often happy to get some rest and are even relieved to be away from their pups' constant demands. "But Honey isn't really a mother to the kittens," I'd pointed out, and Phoebe just smiled her mysterious smile and touched Honey gently on the head.

"She's their mama, all right, Beanie, that's for sure, but Honey and the kittens should be fine for tonight. I read that some mama dogs are happy not to bother with the little ones after a while. That doesn't mean that the babies aren't loved or anything like that, just that there are mama dogs who don't want to be mamas for life."

I'd thought about that then, picturing my own mother, and knowing that, no matter how crabby and tired she was, she'd always want to be my mom and always care for me. I figured that was a pretty good thing.

CHAPTER TWENTY-SIX

Each time Edwin took Honey for a walk, he always had to tempt her with a healthy snack of some kind, usually a slice of cantaloupe or salted carrot. Tonight I held out one of the vanilla wafers I'd stored in my pocket from dinner. The raspberry Fiber One bar would be saved for later.

Honey's tail thumped at the sight of the cookie, and she struggled to her feet as I started to walk away, the cookie in my extended hand and Phoebe taking up the rear, pushing on the big dog's bottom to urge her along. When we made it all the way to the front door, Honey swiped the cookie out of my hand with a corner of her tongue and then nudged me with her barrel head, begging for another.

"There's more where that came from," I whispered into her elephant ear. "I'll give you one when we make it all the way out the house."

A glistening glob of drool hung from Honey's mouth and her black nose twitched. She blinked and I had the sudden urge to give her a hug but there was no time for sentimentality.

The front door creaked as it opened, then closed quietly behind, and I tried to pull Honey down the porch. She objected by shaking her head and then showering me with a downpour of saliva. I wiped off my dripping face with my sweatshirt sleeve, but when Phoebe started to laugh, I had to kick her in the shins in order to keep her quiet. Big mistake. I must have tripped on a step because the next thing I knew, I was flat on the ground, my elbow throbbing. Honey, clearly concerned, planted on paw on my chest and started to yowl.

"Shh, shh, I'm okay, Honey, please be quiet." Thinking and acting quickly, I whipped out another cookie from my pocket and then another. The yowling stopped.

"You're bleeding, Beanie!" Phoebe cried out, forgetting to be quiet.

"Shhh," I told her, index finger to my mouth. "Edwin will hear you." Was it my imagination or did I see a light go on and off at Reel Paradise next door? Then a shadow flickering behind some blinds, but then nothing more.

Phoebe clasped her hand over her mouth. "Are you okay? There's blood everywhere!"

I looked down at my elbow and touched the cut gently. It was about an inch long and dotted with tiny pieces of gravel. Speckles of blood oozed down my arm, but I knew that it wasn't anything serious, so just blew on the cut for a second and then wiped it off with the corner of my sweatshirt. "Don't worry," I whispered to Phoebe. "I'll heal up real quick. Can I borrow one of your socks to stop the bleeding?"

Phoebe was wearing a pair of white knee socks that she'd told me went with the black patent leather shoes she carried with one hand. Quickly, she took off one sock and handed it over. As I wrapped the sock around my arm, tucking in one end into a makeshift bandage, Phoebe took off the other one and tossed it into the grass.

"Can't walk around looking like a weirdo," she said softly, tightening the plaid bandanna she wore as a belt around her waist. "Wearing one sock might make us stand out."

I couldn't help smiling to myself. Phoebe was decked out for our adventure in a red polka-dot skirt and a purple halter top made out of some iridescent material. All was finished off with the yellow, blue, and red bandanna belt and a yellow cardigan sweater. One sock or not, she would certainly be noticeable, but that was the least of our problems.

"We'd better go," I said, popping up from the ground, Phoebe's sock tied securely around my arm. "We'll miss the ferry's docking if we don't hurry." So the two of us scrambled out the front gate, Honey shuffling behind, and headed slowly down the bluff past Reel Paradise, the other bluff Victorians, the eerie, abandoned construction site, Coastal Convenience, around the harbor curve, until we could see the lights of the ferry on the ocean beyond, heading toward the Rock Haven dock. And when I say slowly, I mean slowly. Every single one of Honey's steps took forever, and she seemed to slide backward when Phoebe and I tried to pull her ahead. The big dog was clearly fascinated by each blade of grass, pebble, inch of dirt in her path, stopping to sniff, lick, and sometimes chew with gusto. When we finally reached the long ferry ramp, she was breathing heavily, and Phoebe and I were both perspiring.

I turned to ask Phoebe if she'd brought the bottle of water we'd planned, and I noticed that she was doubled over, her curved back toward me and trembling from head to toe. I put my hand on her shoulder, and she shook her head without looking up. "Don't," she hiccuped, "don't touch me. It'll only make it worse."

"Phoebe, please don't worry. Try to calm down. Everything will be all right, I promise. Maybe you should go back home to Beach Bluff and let me take care of Sam on my own. I'm okay with taking care of everything by myself." But she just shook her head, trembling even more. And finally, to my relief, she slowly stood up again. It was then that I realized that my friend hadn't been sobbing or overtaken by fear, but was laughing hysterically, tears running down her cheeks. Her face was beet red, and I could tell that she was trying to take deep breaths, one at a time.

"I always laugh when I'm really nervous or excited." Phoebe giggled, wiping the tears from her eyes. "Please don't look at me, Beanie. That'll only make me start up again." So we both stood still for a moment, Phoebe covering her face with both hands and heaving with laughter, and me trying to look away, wondering if my friend had finally lost her marbles. Honey, seemingly unconcerned, had spread herself out on the dock, licking each wooden plank as if it was a delicacy.

A few folks started to gather for the ferry's arrival. Someone carrying a small dog in her arms yelled, "Quiet!" as her pup started to bark. I held my breath, hoping not to be recognized and that Honey wouldn't stand up. Somehow, no matter what, she tended to draw attention, and attention was the last thing we needed.

By the time we heard the ferry's horn, Phoebe had settled down and Honey had begun to snore, having fallen asleep mid-lick, her pink tongue still smashed against the splintered dock. Her belly rose with every breath and then fell down again in a tumble of raspy hums. Funny to remember that just a few weeks ago, I'd been frightened of Honey and I'd even thought of her as a monster. Now, of course, I knew how gentle she really was, her silvery coat draping her body in folds, her paws, twice the size of my hands, quivering as she breathed, their black pads soft as velvet and her claws curved like the fingernails of fairy tale giants. And her broad chest, marked with that pure bloom of white and rugged with power, reminded me of her animal strength. It was easy to forget how strong Honey actually was, her gentle nature disguising the muscles that rippled her shoulders in thick, twisted ropes.

Thank goodness that Lola Peterson's mother wasn't working the ferry and I didn't know any of the passengers waiting to board. Two crewmen raced by us up the transfer bridge, one looking back at Honey to moo loudly, something I found just rude. Honey may have been unusually large, but she still had her pride. After all, Edwin had told me that mastiffs' ancestors had once fought lions in ancient Rome, something I found a little hard to believe as I watched the big girl snoring away, pearly foam bubbling from her nose.

I'd been so nervous about getting the three of us out of Beach Bluff without Edwin noticing and then making it all the way to the dock without being seen, there hadn't been time to worry about Sam. Now that we had a few minutes of quiet as we waited for the arriving passengers to exit the ferry, I could hear my own teeth chattering despite the evening's warmth. It was the kind of night where you can only see a slice of moon behind the fog and then everything looks blurry. This was the moment when right and wrong became blurry too, when I was confused about what to do. How would I pretend to be someone I wasn't? Would I keep Sam's dogfighting money after Phoebe videoed the sale?

I looked at Phoebe's pinched face as she watched the crew open the latched ferry door and then at Honey sleeping below. Both were my friends, both had become important to me, but neither one was family. My brother needed me, despite Phoebe, Honey, despite all the other dogs in the world.

It was hard to make out the arriving passengers' faces in the dark as they began to walk down the ramp, and my heart raced. Finding Sam wasn't going to be easy, since I had no idea what he looked like, so I might just have to wait for him to find me once he spied the big dog. I could see Phoebe biting her fingernails, one hand after the other. For a second, I thought about grabbing my friend and running off into the night, never to see Sam or think about dogfighting ever again. But I knew that I really didn't have a choice.

There were never many people on the last ferry to Rock

Haven from America and this group of passengers was no different. Only fifteen folks or so walked out of the boat down the ramp: a blonde, skinny woman with a short, plump man beside her and some real tall guy with a black beard, talking loudly on his cell phone. Sam? Maybe not. He was speaking and walking too quickly without glancing our way. Next, a group of what looked like teenagers; a small elderly man in a suit and tie and carrying a briefcase; a redheaded woman with wild, curly hair; and an enormous man, tall as he was wide, stuffed into a sleeveless muscle shirt. When I noticed a black snake tattoo curling around his fleshy upper arm, I nudged Phoebe with my elbow.

It began to mist, then to rain.

Phoebe was already staring at the snake tattoo, and when the man suddenly stopped to look around, I clutched her hand. As he broke into a run toward us, I thought I might puke. Then he ran right past us to a woman carrying a baby and swept them up in a hug.

A few more kids came down the ramp with their parents following, then a woman on crutches, and then nobody else.

"It's got to be him," Phoebe whispered, nodding to the small man in a suit who was lingering by the road. "He's the only one still here. I'm going to check him out." And then she was off, prancing down the dock boardwalk as if to a party. But when a taxi pulled up and the man hopped in, Phoebe glanced back at me and we both shrugged. She looked so little to me then—a small figure alone at the edge of a boardwalk in the rain.

I felt a rush of relief wash over me then. Sam wasn't coming after all, and although we wouldn't be able to catch him, Phoebe, Honey, and I were all safe. No painful decisions would have to be made and we could all go back to life as usual. I exhaled a long sigh as Phoebe started to walk back toward me. But then, as she came closer and closer, I remembered that my brilliant plan had failed. We may have been safe, but there were dogs who were still suffering, and I couldn't help a single one. And any possibility of getting bail money was gone.

A few members of the ferry crew hung back to prepare the boat for departure, and one of them smiled at me as he looped a rope around his shoulder, as if getting ready to lasso a calf.

"Kind of late for you to be out, isn't it?" he asked, eyes lowered. "Why don't you come inside the ticket office for a few minutes, at least until the rain stops. Are your parents coming to pick you up soon?"

To my surprise, Honey suddenly raised up her head and growled. And then I remembered what I'd always known before: Honey wasn't just a pet, but a guard dog, an animal bred to protect those she loved from harm. I turned to look at her and a hand gripped my shoulder from behind. When I spun around, the crewman's face stared back at me, his plump cheeks a rosy pink, reminding me of a child left out in the cold. But his eyes really creeped me out; two slits of black, sunken deep into his head. His hair was shaved at the sides and highlighted blond at the tips, and when he grinned, I shivered, head to toe.

"All's good, guys," he called back to the other crewmen, all the time pushing me forward. "I'm just going to pick up this dog to take back to the mainland. My folks at home bought him to be bred. Be back in a sec."

And so Sam the dogman had found us after all. He ushered Honey and me into the ticket office, hand still on my back, kicking the door open with one foot, then shoving me inside. Honey followed quietly, but I could see the hair on her neck stand up, and she slid between Sam and me, her whole body on alert. I looked around for Phoebe, who was nowhere to be found, but then I saw her white face peering through the open window, looking right back at me. I startled, then took a deep breath as she quickly pressed a finger to her mouth. Luckily, Sam's back was toward her so he couldn't see a thing, and when she bent forward to hold up her cell phone, I began to tremble like a leaf.

"I shouldn't pay you a single dollar," Sam hissed into my face. "You told me you were an adult. I work for professionals, and we don't mess with dumb little kids."

Honey raised her head up higher. Next I heard a rumble from her throat. And then Sam reached quickly into his jacket pocket and pulled out a wad of bills. "But if I don't fork over the cash, you'll probably just go straight to the cops. And all this bother just for a dumb, ugly dog."

His rotten breath curdled every corner of the room.

I saw the ticket booth's glass counter, I saw the pine beadboard lining the wall, I saw a poster of Hermit Beach, the ocean and the jetties just beyond.

I saw my brother's hands on his first fishing rod, his face lit with joy. I heard his voice in my ear, quiet and calm. And suddenly, pretending to be someone I wasn't didn't seem possible anymore. My carefully-thought-out plan to trick Sam flew out the window.

"I know who you are," I said shakily to Sam, "and I am going to make sure you don't hurt animals anymore. I know all the horrible things you do to dogs. So your stupid money is nothing but trash to me. Take it all back and leave all the innocent dogs alone."

I couldn't believe that my words had taken over my mouth but felt myself stretch taller and taller as I spoke.

Sam roared like a wild animal with a terrible wound, and he seemed to triple in size right before my eyes.

"Why you little . . . Who do you think you are, messing with me? You don't know anything about anything, you stupid kid. We've been in the business for years without being caught, so you'd better shut your mouth, or you'll be sorry, I can promise you that." His body lurched from one side to the other, and I could almost feel its heat as he lunged ahead in my direction.

And then I saw Honey rise up and calmly clamp Sam's right arm with her jaws. I could tell that she hadn't bitten him but was simply taking control.

Green bills fluttered all over the office, flying over Sam's face as he stumbled to the floor and then, to my amazement, Honey sunk herself down on the dogman's legs so he couldn't move.

"Good girl, Honey," I called to her, in a shaky voice I didn't recognize as my own. "Good girl."

I could hear the dogman yelling and saw his face turn white, then red, then white again, but I couldn't understand what he was saying. Honey was barking too loud.

Then the door flew open, Phoebe running inside. She was holding her cell phone in front of her like a sword, sobbing and smiling at the same time. She pointed the camera right at Sam's face as she spoke. "Are you okay, Bean, are you hurt? I think I got what we need on my phone! And, believe me, I was ready to jump right into the room if that man laid a hand on either you or Honey. Sure hope I got everything we needed—my hand was shaking a bunch."

I looked down at Sam, who was still struggling to get up from under Honey's weight, and then at the money strewn all over the room. There it was right in front of me, all the cash I needed. I could keep it for bail and help my brother go free, but it was blood money, making me gag from its stench.

The big dog panted, tears collecting in the ruffles of her face. Maybe just from all her huffing and puffing but maybe from something else too. She was still sitting on Sam, who'd begun whining to be let free.

"Your dog isn't even worth one cent, but call her off and I'll leave you alone. I can always find another stupid mutt."

An invisible shield dropped over my chest. I knew that no one else could see it but I couldn't care less. Finally, my own coat of arms, who I really was. Willis was my brother but would have a future once he'd paid for his crime. Honey was strong as all get out, no doubt about that, yet she didn't have any say in her own life. The big dog had taken care of the abandoned kittens as if they were her own, and I would guard her from a life of sorrow the way she was guarding me now.

And all the other animals who needed my help.

"Call the police," I told Phoebe quietly. "Call 911. Tell them we've caught a criminal and we need to get our dog home."

And then I turned back to Sam, hands on my hips. "You'll never get Honey," I said, spitting out each word, "and you'll never hurt another animal again."

CHAPTER TWENTY-SEVEN

Naturally, my mother had plenty to say the next morning. The sheriff filled her and Edwin in the night before, after driving Phoebe and Honey back to Beach Bluff and then me all the way home. I guess Sam was taken to the jail to be questioned and Phoebe gave the police her phone with the video recording.

I was too tired to say much as I stumbled through the door, and my mother too shocked to take it all in.

But when I woke at daybreak, scared by a nightmare about a ship of mastiffs sinking at sea, she was sitting on Willis's bed, staring at me with a frightened look on her face. Then, without a word, she got up and left the room to make an early breakfast of fried eggs and toast, something she hadn't done in a long time, apparently taking a rare morning off from work. It wasn't until I had finished eating and gotten dressed that she finally spoke her mind.

At first, my mother was mad, then teary, then mad all over again. As a punishment, I'd been ordered to help her clean out the basement, and when her outburst began, I knew I was in for it. She was still ranting and raving as we lugged two plastic bins of laundry up the narrow basement stairs to my bedroom.

"You should have come to me, Bean," my mother said, a bit out of breath, watching me drop a pile of clean T-shirts and jeans on my bed. "For goodness' sake, why didn't you come to me? Maybe I could have helped. It's good to be independent, but you can't always handle everything by yourself."

"I wanted to tell you."

"But you didn't. You did not. Haven't we had enough trouble around here without you getting all mixed up with actual criminals? I know that your impulse to help Willis was well intended, but you're lucky you didn't end up in a predicament that could have affected the rest of your life. You know, you can't rescue everyone and every single dog."

Tears sprung to my eyes. Not because my mother was angry, but because I needed to believe that I could save the animals, at least that it was important to try. I just wasn't ready to give up on that.

"But I suppose that I admire your guts," my mother continued, "and your determination to make things better. Just please keep your side of the street clean and try to stay out of trouble. The fact is that we all need to accept what can't be changed."

I wasn't sure what keeping "my side of the street clean" exactly meant, but chances were that I wasn't doing it. And believing that things couldn't change was exactly what I would not accept, no matter what. Then, to my own surprise, I suddenly let out what I'd been holding in for so long, as if my words marched out of my mouth on their very own. "The truth is that I miss us being a real family, Mom, the four of us together again, and I'm angry that we don't have a father any-more and that Willis is gone too. You're always working and never say anything about either of them, or how they just left us behind. And you let Willis sit in jail when I needed him most. I'm sick of things that need to be different left as okay. Maybe sometimes trouble can help make stuff right again."

"Oh, Bean," my mother said, and then she said it all over again. "Oh, Bean." She looked like a child for a minute, her hair in a ponytail and her worn blue sweatshirt full of stains and holes. But it was her expression that killed me: Her sadness churned and slid down her face like butter off a plate, the bitter-ness that usually held her together melting in front of my eyes.

And then, out of the blue, my mother pulled me close. "I miss your father too," she said softly, "but it was his decision to leave. Your brother is a different matter altogether and I would do anything to change what's happened to him. I just, for the life of me, can't figure out what to do or how to help; this whole thing, his arrest, jail, his crime, has really thrown me for a loop. I'm sorry, Bean. I'm sorry that I haven't been stronger for you, and I promise to find the courage to take you to see Willis soon. I should have gone to see him with you earlier, when this whole mess began. I guess parents don't always do what's right."

We stood there together under my bedroom window, the curtains drawn open again, and I inhaled her scent: laundry bleach and Fruity Pebbles, sharp and sweet.

My mother may not have been perfect, and my entire fam-ily was kind of a mess, but when I thought of Phoebe's parents,

I realized that I really had it pretty good. The past was the past, all that'd gone wrong before, yet I knew I could move forward, no matter what. My father had abandoned us, but my mother still loved me and my brother would always be there for us, even when miles away. Although Willis would be gone for a year, I'd be fine on my own, and I had his tools stored safely away where I could find them when needed. While I still didn't know how to fix everything all by myself, I'd learned how to try. And "it is what it is" would never be my deal. I would always fight for my own truth.

CHAPTER TWENTY-EIGHT

I ran into Sheriff Cobbs at Coastal Convenience a day later and she told me that Sam had been shipped off to America and would be questioned until the matter was resolved. She also said that the video Phoebe made would be a big help getting him charged, but for heaven's sake, it had been way too dangerous to meet with the dogman all on our own. The good news was that the Massachusetts state police had already gone to the property where Sam lived and rescued five German shepherds that had been chained outside.

The soda I'd been drinking fizzled in my mouth, and I almost spit it out thinking about the poor German shepherds. Not exactly "really good news" to my mind. But then, for some reason, the cover of Phoebe's book *Heidi* came to mind, and I pictured the rescued German shepherds sitting on top of some green hill as they proudly watched over all the animals in the valley below. A breeze ruffled their downy fur. They shook their heads, waiting to guide their flock home.

But what about that horrible dog convention where Sam had been heading and the dogs that would suffer there? With or without Sam, I was pretty sure that the convention would go on. The sheriff told me not to focus on the negative but to remember how many dogs I'd already helped save, and that tips from all over the East Coast were still coming in.

"You remind me of your brother." She smiled half-heartedly, offering me a chip from the bag of Doritos she'd just bought. "Smart but stubborn as all get out. You and your friend could have gotten hurt or even worse. I'm sorry I didn't listen to you more carefully when you came to talk to me before, Bean, but you can't go around chasing criminals at the age of eleven. On the other hand, I commend you for your courage and for standing up for what's right." Then Sheriff Cobbs shook my hand, just like I was someone real important, and gave me a funny little salute.

I watched as she left Coastal, making her way through the crowd, and understood what I'd never realized before. Our sheriff was definitely tiny, no doubt about that, but she cut a very wide path.

Edwin took Phoebe and me into town that night to celebrate Sam's arrest. He was dressed in his usual shorts and button-down shirt, but he wore sandals, thank goodness, instead of his worn slippers. I tried to avoid looking at his feet since his toes were sweaty and sprouted wiry hair, but when he linked arms with Phoebe and me, I could tell that he was really enjoying himself. Naturally, he had to go and embarrass the two of us by breaking out into the traditional Australian national anthem for the whole town to hear. I bet he googled it on his laptop that very morning, just to torture us when the time was right.

We all ate double-scooped mint–chocolate chip ice-cream cones after lunch, and Edwin bought Phoebe and me matching red baseball caps with little white dogs on the visors. We played a few games of Skee-Ball in the arcade, then I beat both of their brains out at ring toss. When it started to rain, we dashed over to the carousel for cover, and I realized my new hat had been lost, maybe blown off in the wind. Phoebe let me wear hers as I watched her mount a green beat-up plaster horse.

I thought that carousels were cool, especially ours in Rock Haven, but I didn't feel like riding that particular day. After all, I wasn't really a child anymore, so I just hung back and looked for Phoebe as she went round and round.

Seeing the old, dented carousel and all the kids reminded me of when I was a little kid myself. Before Willis had ever been arrested and before I knew about dogfighting or that animals had souls.

CHAPTER TWENTY-NINE

As it turned out, Phoebe's parents never made it to Rock Haven that summer, and on the last day of the month, they sent word that she would have to leave the island to return home the following week. At first, this made me really angry since Phoebe's parents had promised and promised to come, and I just didn't think it was fair. Phoebe had been so excited about them visiting, and I hated to see her disappointed again. And I couldn't stand the thought of my friend leaving earlier than expected.

But Phoebe was pretty chill about the whole thing, telling me that there was no point in getting upset like she did the last time her parents bailed.

"Mother and Father are always changing their plans," she told me as we walked over to Lookout Point the morning before she left. "So I kind of expected it. No point in my being down in the dumps all over again because being down in the dumps really stinks. I'd much rather spend today with you looking for seals and counting all the ducks on the water."

Then she assured me that she'd call when she got to Providence and be back the following summer. "Don't be sad, Beanie," she said, patting my arm. "Maybe you could come visit me and Honey, or I could come stay with you for some weekend at your house. Providence isn't really all that far away."

I knew that Providence wasn't far, but I doubted Phoebe's parents would let her visit me in Rock Haven over the winter and knew it would be too expensive for me to visit her.

Phoebe wanted to spend one last afternoon at the Point before she left, but the day we chose was what the old-timers called soupy: the fog so thick you could almost eat it with a spoon. But Phoebe was determined to try to see the seals since they often crawled onto the rocks for warmth this time of year. I'd already seen two big ones that summer, sunning themselves on the beach and honking like nobody's business. And there was something about seal eyes that made you like the critters from the get-go. Liquidy and black with long lashes that batted madly. It was impossible not to smile when faced with an eyelash-batting seal.

Phoebe told me she'd been up late the night before reading all about how seals were unlike any other water creature and that seal pups can survive on their own after only four weeks. Dog puppies, she reported, weren't really ready to leave their mothers until eight weeks, kittens a little longer, and humans, well, that was another matter entirely. "Human babies and children," Phoebe told me drowsily, "always need their parents."

We only spent a few minutes at the Lookout that morning. It was chilly and impossible to see anything below, or even our own feet. All we could do was hold on to each other for warmth and hope that the murky weather would pass.

The day that Phoebe left Rock Haven, she'd selected a very grown-up outfit to wear. In fact, when I first saw her standing on Beach Bluff's front porch, there was a minute when I didn't even recognize her.

She had on a pink silk shawl, most likely from one of her mother's trunks, paired with an off-white skirt that I'd seen her wear before. Her plastic beads and silver cowboy boots were nowhere to be found. A simple gold chain hung around her neck, and a pair of plain tan flats were on her feet.

When it was time to go, I hugged her, and we both looked over at Honey, who had joined us for the farewell. As usual, she was snoring, fast asleep on the row of plump striped cushions Edwin had left for her on the porch floor. The kittens were lined up—three black-and-white dots on a giant's silver back, and Phoebe leaned down to kiss each of them. Next we both patted Honey's head, then immediately wiped off our faces after the big dog burped and sneezed.

"Don't be sad, Bean," Phoebe pleaded, looking at my alarmed expression when the taxi driver beeped her horn impatiently. "It's okay. Don't worry about me. I'm used to change, different nannies, sometimes different schools, even apartments and houses. One year, Mother and Father decided that moving to another country might be nice and I thought to myself, well, that's okay, I guess I could get used to that. But then they figured it would be better if the two of them went ahead to scout out some places, you know, while I stayed home in Providence for a few months. But they came back for Christmas, and as it turned out, we never ended up moving anyway. So you see, I know how to let things and people go. It always works out one way or another. I'm used to it."

The lump in my throat was so big that I couldn't speak. Phoebe might have been used to letting go, but I was not.

I wasn't going to cry and then I did cry, just for a bit. We stood there together, neither of us saying a word, Phoebe patting my arm awkwardly. I could see that she understood I was embarrassed.

"Here, Bean, this is for you. I want you to keep it," Phoebe insisted suddenly, pushing one of her Altoids boxes into my hand. "Just something to remember me by. And I promise that I didn't sneak in any of my great-grandmother's teeth."

And then we both laughed until we couldn't anymore.

I swallowed hard and waved as she slipped into the taxi and then shook Edwin's hand good-bye. He was loading up the car with as many suitcases as could fit. "Honey and all the rest will be shipped to Providence later this evening," he told me, slamming shut the trunk door. "Stay out of trouble, *mate*, and keep all the animals safe from harm."

I nodded and opened the tin box in my hand. A tiny china silver dog and a black cat inside.

EPILOGUE

My mother and I visited Willis at the Nook School in Maine twice during the coming year and attended his graduation that spring.

Nook turned out to be a pretty okay place and didn't look anything like a real school. The students lived together on this little farm and they had all kinds of chores. Willis told me that he had to muck out the stables each morning and help care for a bunch of critters, including goats, sheep, pigs, two horses, and one fat brown-and-white cow. He seemed to like it at Nook and had a whole new group of friends, definitely different than the ones he'd had at home. I can't really tell you how, but they seemed pretty okay from what I saw during our visits. I figured I better start being more careful about assumptions. Sometimes the real truth ended up different from what you first understand and assuming stuff can lead to no good.

I could tell that Willis had changed, and not just because he'd grown a scruffy beard. He was kinda quieter and didn't laugh as much as before. But he still grinned when I cracked one of my stupid jokes and still wrestled me to the floor. My brother hadn't grown taller, thank goodness for that, but now he had these arm muscles that popped up under his shirt.

When I told him I wanted to start lifting weights so I could have big guns just like him, he shook his head and frowned.

"You're too young for lifting, sis. Just stick to what you're good at. You know, hanging out at Lookout Point and fishing with your pals." I didn't say anything then but felt a bang in my chest. Willis still saw me as a little kid and it hurt my feelings that he couldn't tell I'd already grown muscles where he couldn't see. I started to scratch an itchy spot on my wrist and looked down at it carefully. Only a small, plain old mosquito bite and not a hive at all. Thinking about it, I hadn't had a single hive since deciding to stand up to Sam. Or vertigo either. Maybe speaking my mind really did "serve me well," as Sheriff Cobbs had said.

While Willis didn't get admitted to Harvard University, Boston College offered him a full ride. I knew that my brother was disappointed about Harvard, but I could also tell that he didn't want my mother or me to see how he felt. Funny, it wasn't until my brother returned from Nook that I realized Willis was pretty good at hiding his real feelings. Sometimes, it's better to just blurt out the truth, no matter how scary it might be.

I guess I might have as much to teach my brother as he taught me.

Honey's kittens found homes with families in Rock Haven, all preapproved by Phoebe, of course, and the big dog needed to have a new family as well, since Phoebe's parents decided, once they returned to Providence, that they didn't want such a large animal in the city. I wasn't exactly shocked.

"You must be kidding me," my mother said, when I first asked her if I could keep Honey. "We barely have room for the two of us. Times are hard, Bean, especially with Willis going on to college, scholarship or not."

Phoebe called me when she got home to say that her parents finally made it back to Providence. She also told me that Edwin had gone to visit his daughter in North Dakota for a week but had already signed on as her nanny for another year. Apparently, he'd also auditioned for one of those big-time cooking shows on TV, although hadn't made the final cut.

Phoebe and I continued calling each other for a while and even made plans for a bunch of visits, but never managed to pull them off. It turned out that her parents enrolled her in some language arts camp for the following summer so she wouldn't be able to return to Beach Bluff after all. Slowly, the phone calls stopped, and we eventually lost touch, although a small box from her arrived at Christmas. When I opened it, I had to laugh: a silver framed photograph of my friend holding a little white dog. The name Helen of Troy was written neatly in red ink on a slip of paper attached with tape.

At the end of August, Reel Paradise had been boarded up the way it was every year, and I never got to tell Mr. Spencer good-bye. I wondered where he went during the winter months and if his ankle ever healed.

The construction site at the end of the bluff got shut down by the town council, the football player's house never finished. Towanda from Coastal told me that the mayor wanted to have a garden planted there, but I knew that a bunch of flowers and bushes could never fill that giant hole.

Sheriff Cobbs kept me in the loop whenever she learned anything new about dogfighting gangs. So far there'd been thirty dogs rescued from all over, not including the German shepherds she'd already told me about. And Sam had been arrested, a full investigation underway.

"It will be a long process," the sheriff cautioned me, "and a challenging one at that, so we'll have to be patient, but I promise that we'll never give up."

Beach Bluff was rented by some large family from New York for the rest of the summer, then boarded up for the winter. I stopped going over to the bluff for a while, since my friends and I mostly just hung out around the lagoon. But I knew that I'd never walk past Phoebe's old house again without remembering that month when we became friends and found our voices hidden deep in the wall.

Right before I go to sleep each night, I think about my brother and wonder if he'll ever live back home again. Maybe he will and maybe he won't, but at least he's free.

Sometimes, if I'm feeling really lonely, I'll open my window and listen to the sound of foghorns mixed in with waves lapping the shore. Then I'll go lie down in Willis's bed, squeezing in under the jumble of covers next to my own enormous animal, my magnificent guard dog, Honey Wright.

ACKNOWLEDGMENTS

Thank you to my remarkable editor, Emily Seife, who read my manuscript with enormous sensitivity. Her many insights, as well as her disciplined eye, often protected Bean from wandering off island into murky and dangerous waters. I am deeply appreciative for this, as well as for Emily's unwavering warmth, humor, and thoughtfulness. She has left her delicate imprint on every page.

I'm also appreciative of the many folks at Scholastic who helped this book come to life: book designer Yaffa Jaskoll; production editor Josh Berlowitz; copyeditor Jody Corbett; proof-reader Jessica White; assistant editor Jeffrey West; as well as Lizette Serrano, Danielle Yadao, and Rachel Feld. Your hard work and many talents are deeply appreciated.

I'm greatly indebted to my two extraordinary daughters, Jennifer and Lisa. You have both taught me what it means to be a mother, its wondrous complexities and joys. Thank you for showing me that Bean and Phoebe must follow their own unique paths.

My agent, Ginger Knowlton, has represented me with loyalty and enthusiasm. Her vast experience in publishing, as well as her warmth and efficiency, has been invaluable. Thank you, Ginger, for all your hard work.

And to Annabelle, whose heart was as large as her jowls.

ABOUT THE AUTHOR

Denise Gosliner Orenstein is a graduate of Bennington College and Brown University. Her career in education includes teaching at American University in Washington, DC, as well as in bush villages throughout the state of Alaska. Additionally, she has cooked for an Alaskan village prison, worked as a PEN prison writing mentor, taught literature classes, and assisted in a canine-therapy program for inmates. Most recently, as head of a school for children with learning differences, she introduced a curriculum based on two rescued Shetland ponies, and she currently volunteers as part of a canine-therapy team with her dog, Lily. Denise is the author of five books for children and young adults, including *Dirt* and *A Guard Dog Named Honey*, and is the mother of two daughters.